HARLEY HITCH

AND THE IRON FOREST

HARLEY HITCH

AND THE IRON FOREST

VASHTI HARDY

ILLUSTRATED BY

GEORGE ERMOS

■ SCHOLASTIC

Published in the UK by Scholastic Children's Books, 2021
Euston House, 24 Eversholt Street, London, NW1 1DB, UK
A division of Scholastic Limited.

Scholastic Ltd Ireland offices at:
Unit 89E, Lagan Road, Dublin Industrial Estate, Glasnevin, Dublin 11.

London – New York – Toronto – Sydney – Auckland
Mexico City – New Delhi – Hong Kong

ISBN 978 0702 30255 8

A CIP catalogue record for this book is available from the British Library.

Printed by CPI Group (UK) Ltd, Croydon, CR0 4YY
Papers used by Scholastic Children's Books are made
from wood grown in sustainable forests.

1 3 5 7 9 10 8 6 4 2

www.scholastic.co.uk

For Elana

JUNKYARD of FORGOTTEN
MACHINE DREAMS

THE
IRON FOREST

OLD MILL

RUSTY RIVER

★ STAR CHATTER
OBSERVATORY

COPPER MOUNTAINS

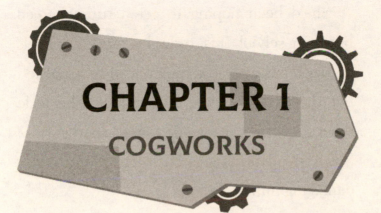

CHAPTER 1
COGWORKS

Harley ran up the lane towards Cogworks, puffing like the Inventia Express. The school was located at the top of a hill, which was not a good thing when you were late.

Sprocket, her robot dog, zoomed ahead. He was twice as fast as her, having been fitted with turbo legs only a month ago.

"Wait for me!" she called.

He stopped and tilted his head, as though to

say, "Is everything all right?"

She'd been hoping to get a turbocharged boost to school this term by putting wheels on her boots and attaching a lead to Sprocket, but the first time she had tried it, the little robot's circuits overloaded and sparks flew. She'd mended his legs but didn't want to risk damaging him again.

Harley glanced up at Cogworks. The morning sun glinted on the twisting steel pipes, the great domed roof and tall, layered towers of the classroom and laboratory block.

The enormous cog clock above the entrance read one minute to nine – she would just make it. As she ran, Fenelda Spiggot's familiar smug pose, silhouetted in one of the windows, caught her attention: hands on hips and sharply cut bobbed hair. Harley grimaced and charged onwards, hoping Fenelda hadn't spotted her.

But as she approached the school gates, a loud roar erupted behind her, along with the frantic honk of a horn. Just in time, Harley looked over her shoulder to see a shiny silver transporter heading straight towards her.

"Out of the way!" someone called from inside the vehicle.

Harley had no choice but to leap into the bank of thistles at the side of the lane. The transporter whooshed past, spraying dirt as it made its way through the gates into the

Cogworks grounds.

Harley groaned. The driver had clearly seen her yet had expected her to jump out of the way! Now not only was she late, she was also covered in dirt. Her temper began rolling like a small thunderstorm in her chest. This wasn't a good start to the day. Sprocket bounded back towards her and licked her cheek with his cold metal tongue.

"I'm fine, thank you," she said to him as she rolled back on to her knees. She looked towards the transporter and would have paused to admire the sleek metal body and chrome wheels if she hadn't been so cross at being forced off the road. "Hey! You need to be more careful!"

With a backfire chug, the transporter sped down the other side of the hill, having deposited a boy on the school steps.

The clock began to chime nine.

Sprocket whined sadly and Harley patted him on the nose. "I know, late again." She stood up and brushed herself down. "You'd better head home. I'll see you after school."

A mechanical voice sounded as she passed the school gates. "Two minutes past nine. Late attendance will not be tolerated."

Harley stopped and looked back as the gatekeeper robot, Primbot, stepped from behind one of the pillars, wagging a metal finger at her. Harley was certain Professor Fretshaw had made this robot particularly tall just so the robot, too, could tower over the students and look intimidating. In fact, now she thought of it, Primbot did look remarkably like the head teacher herself. Harley quashed her anger and put on her best smile. "You must've seen what just happened. It wasn't my fault!"

Primbot shook her head. "You must leave extra time to allow for delays."

Harley wrinkled her nose. She had aimed to leave earlier, but Sprocket had been especially playful this morning and then she'd wanted to help Grandpa Eden water the strawberries. Even so, she would have been just in time – if it hadn't been for that transporter. She looked at Primbot and tried another smile. "You could let me off. It is the first day of term."

Primbot tapped a screen on her chest. It flashed up with the words *Harley Hitch – LATE*. They folded into a virtual envelope and shot away with a whoosh.

Harley scowled and stomped towards the school, calling behind her, "Why are you even wearing glasses? You're a robot – your eyesight is perfect!"

The boy at the top of the steps stared at Harley. Curly brown hair completely covered one of his eyes and his other eye blinked at her several times behind thick black-rimmed glasses. He was dressed in the Cogworks uniform of a white shirt with leather cuffs, a black waistcoat with a cog badge on the pocket, black trousers, and a hip tool belt. It was all perfectly pressed and new.

Harley glanced down at her big brown boots, pleated skirt and waistcoat, all adapted with many pockets and buckles to hold her useful tools. Her shirt, which had been white this morning, was now covered in dirt and prickles from jumping into the bushes. It wasn't fair; she'd tried so hard to get here on time, to stay out of trouble, and now it was all ruined. She felt a sudden surge of dislike towards the boy. He had been dropped off by the transporter; this was all his fault.

The boy gave a nervous smile.

Harley's lips tightened. "You made me late!" She scowled, then noticed the worried expression on the boy's face and remembered what Grandpa Eden always said: if your boiler is about to blow, hold your breath and count to ten. If it still wants to boil, then you can let it out.

The boy pushed his glasses up the bridge of his nose with a shaking hand, and they slid back down again. "I'm sorry about my mum, she's always in a hurry... Are you all right? You're going a bit puffy-cheeked," he said nervously.

Harley observed the boy as she finished counting. He was timid and probably wouldn't have meant to run her off the road himself. She sucked in a breath. "Ten!" No, she decided, she still wasn't all right. "Being in a hurry is not an excuse!" She folded her arms.

The boy looked down at his polished shoes.

"My mum was rushing to get to her new job."

"I have no idea how she didn't see me until the last moment."

"Perhaps it was on account of your…"

Harley narrowed her eyes and tilted her head. "On account of my…?"

"Err … your hair," he said hesitantly. "It blends in with the…" He waved his finger as though it would help to find the right word.

"Bushes?" She raised her eyebrows. "You were going to say bushes, weren't you?" She supposed her hair did match the bushes pretty perfectly. She pulled a twig from it and threw it over her shoulder. "I choose a different colour each term. Me and my grandpa Eden like to experiment. This green uses a combination of sorrel roots, spinach, peppermint leaves and snapdragons."

The boy looked at her with nervous interest. "It's … nice."

Harley tilted her head and considered. "So, you're new?"

"Yes. We just moved from Inventia City."

"What's your name?"

"Cosmo."

"Where do you live?"

"Hinge Street."

"What class are you in?"

"I don't know. I need to report to Professor Fretshaw first."

Harley gave a shiver. "Boy, does she have it in for me. Do you know, she once told me off for asking too many questions?"

"Really?" Cosmo said, a slight smile playing around his lips.

"No loitering, Harley Hitch," Primbot said as she clunked up the steps and into the building. She looked to Cosmo. "Cosmo Willoughby, please report to Professor Fretshaw."

"Has our new pupil arrived?" called a shrill voice from behind a door in the entrance hall. A voice that Harley recognized: Professor Fretshaw. Harley ducked inside and ran to the great iron staircase, hoping she wouldn't be spotted. The stairs began trundling upwards in a spiral on the inside of a tower like an escalator. Harley was looking forward to being in her new class. Professor Spark had always seemed friendly when Harley had seen her around school before, so Harley hurried along the corridor to her new classroom, hoping she could sneak in the back before the end of the register.

As Harley crept into the room, Fenelda

Spiggot's hand shot into the air. "Professor Spark, Harley Hitch is late."

Everybody turned to face her and Professor Spark looked up, her large brown eyes making contact with Harley's. The professor had voluminous, tight-curled hair and wore a navy dress emblazoned with shooting stars, constellations and moons. Harley smiled apologetically, bracing herself for the telling-off.

"It's not even like she needed to be late," continued Fenelda. "I saw her outside chatting, probably because she can't—"

"Thank you for your assessment, Fenelda," Professor Spark interrupted. "Take a seat, please, Harley."

Harley was relieved not to be shouted at in front of the class, but sat down gloomily at the last free desk, which, unfortunately, was behind Fenelda. So much for impressing her new teacher on the first day.

While Professor Spark finished the register, Fenelda turned around and whispered, "Interesting new hairstyle, Harley."

Harley shrugged. "You should try some interesting yourself."

Professor Spark coughed. "Now that we're all here for our first session together, I'd like to get to know you all a little. Professor Fretshaw has passed on notes about each of you." She gestured to a toppling pile of paper on her desk and frowned. "But I like to make up my own mind." She scooped the pile off the desk and placed it in a cupboard at the back of the room.

Harley straightened in her chair. Professor Fretshaw was not Harley's greatest fan – the feeling was mutual – and no doubt the professor had made that clear in her notes. There was the time Harley had jammed the school generator trying to mend it, and the time she and Rufus had got stuck on the Cogworks clock because she'd invented some wings to try and travel to school faster... But if Professor Spark was giving them all a fresh slate, this could be a chance to prove herself. This might be the year she could get the thing she most desired and had never achieved: Cogworks' Pupil of the Term.

CHAPTER 2

LIQUID LIGHT

Professor Spark strode down the aisle between the desks. "I'd like to get to know you all through your actions. So, I'm going to start with a little assignment."

The class straightened their backs.

"I've noticed that the watermill at—"

Professor Spark was interrupted by a brisk knock on the door which didn't wait for an answer. The head teacher, Professor Fretshaw, stalked into the room.

She was the tallest professor at Cogworks, and thin, as though she had gradually stretched over many years. She wasn't actually that old, so Grandpa Elliot had told Harley, but she frowned often, which gave her mean, wrinkly eyes. She paused and looked back over her shoulder. "Come along, then."

Cosmo stepped inside, chin to his chest so that his curly hair covered most of his face.

"Cosmo Willoughby will be joining you in Spark Class."

"Welcome, Cosmo." Professor Spark beamed warmly. "Do take a seat." She looked around, then gestured to the seat beside Harley.

Harley groaned inwardly; Cosmo's arrival had already caused her problems today, so she didn't want him to sit next to her. Maybe he was the type of person whom trouble followed around, whether they wanted it or not. This was something that Professor Fretshaw had said about her last year; and after the clock incident, no matter how hard Harley tried to impress Professor Fretshaw, she had Harley branded as a troublemaker. Harley glanced at Cosmo. She didn't want to make the same mistake with Professor Spark. Only last week, Harley had promised her grandparents a fresh start for the new school year, and she wasn't going to ruin it on the first day. There was an empty seat at its own table at the front. Maybe Cosmo could sit there. But then Professor Fretshaw fixed her with pin-sharp eyes and, heaving a sigh, Harley pulled out the chair for Cosmo to sit down.

Professor Fretshaw glanced at her electro-pad. "Late on the first day, I see, Harley. And you look as though you've been rolling around in the dirt with that robot dog of yours."

Fenelda sniggered and Harley tightened her jaw.

"I suggest you smarten yourself up at the earliest opportunity." Professor Fretshaw tutted loudly, shook her head and left the room.

"Let's continue," said Professor Spark. "You might have noticed that the watermill at Rusty River is beginning to fall apart. I'd like you to work in pairs to design and make a miniature working model of a new, updated version by the end of the lesson. We have a double period so it should be doable if you work hard. And there's an exciting prospect for the winners."

They all leaned in.

"I will personally take your design to

Forgetown Electrical Company as a proposal, and this would be a step in the right direction for anyone interested in being a contender for Pupil of the Term."

There were a few excited gasps and the class exchanged glances with each other.

"I'm going to let you decide who you partner with. I'll give you a minute."

Harley scanned the room. She would have to choose her working partner carefully; how she wanted that framed Pupil of the Term certificate on her wall and the golden light bulb badge! Her grandpas would be so proud. She thought for a moment. Dolores Dredge was excellent, she'd been Pupil of the Term twice, but she was bossy and would take over. Rufus Digby was fun to work with, but he'd never been Pupil of the Term either and they would giggle too much and get into trouble. Fenelda Spiggot was one of the smartest in the class, three-time Pupil of the Term and the previous winner, but Harley would rather work with a mushroom. Her eyes met with Lettice Bigley's, who was smiling at her from the table in front. Lettice was sensible, and good with tools, like Harley. She'd won once, though that was two years ago so she would be keen to work hard too. Harley stood up.

"Shall we—"

"Letti!" Fenelda declared, hooking Letti's arm. "Yes, I'd love to pair up with you!"

Letti looked over her shoulder and mouthed, *Sorry.* Harley smiled, knowing it wasn't Lettice's fault. She had never been very good at standing up to Fenelda. She would feel bad for not working with Harley, but if Harley made a fuss, Professor Spark might think she was causing trouble.

Fenelda and Harley had been friends once. For the first few years at Cogworks, they'd been put together because they were the cleverest in the class and worked well in a pair. Fenelda had always liked winning things and could sometimes be meaner than Harley liked, but Harley had always pulled her up on it and could hold her own. Then, in year three, Professor Fretshaw had introduced Pupil of the Term. There had been a competition to see who could grow the tallest cogflower, and Harley had won, until Fenelda told Professor Fretshaw that Harley had help from Grandpa Eden. It wasn't true, but Professor Fretshaw wouldn't listen and had disqualified Harley. That was when Harley decided that best friends were too much trouble. If she wanted to succeed, she was better off on her own.

Harley sighed; she would have to team up with Rufus. Even though he didn't take things seriously, he might be willing to try hard on the first day of term. But as she looked around the room, she saw he was with Henry, and that left…

Professor Spark strode over. "Harley, perhaps you could pair up with Cosmo?"

Harley glanced to her side. She had been deliberately ignoring the new boy sitting next to her. His brown curls drooped across one eye. She knew it wasn't really his fault, but she couldn't help blaming him for the way her day had started. Partnering with him was risky; she'd barely met him and had no idea what he was like to work with. She needed to impress

Professor Spark if she was going to be in with a chance at winning.

"Harley?" Professor Spark said a bit more briskly now, frowning.

Well, it didn't look as though she had much of a choice. "Yes, of course, Professor," she said hastily. "Would you like to be my partner, Cosmo?"

He nodded shyly.

The class started planning their designs.

As it turned out, Harley found she was glad she was working with Cosmo after all. He didn't talk too much and seemed happy to follow her ideas. He also had some good thoughts on energy-saving mechanics and became chattier the longer the lesson went on. He was probably feeling nervous about starting at a new school and fitting in, so she felt a little bad for being so rude to him earlier.

Halfway through the lesson, the pair had finished their designs and collected the materials for their prototypes.

"Right, Cosmo, you get what we need from the box of components, and I'll get the liquid light for power."

Harley went to the store cupboard. Fenelda was already in there, gathering what she needed.

"Did I hear you say liquid light? Here, let me pass you some," Fenelda said sweetly. "I hope you didn't mind me pointing out that you were late this morning."

Harley glared flatly. The golden light bulb badge gleamed on Fenelda's waistcoat and Harley imagined how satisfying it would be when Fenelda was forced to hand it over.

"It's just that I'm going to win Pupil of the Term again, so I have to do what I need to do. I'm sure you understand, having won it, let's see…" She paused and moved to count on her fingers, then shrugged. "Never."

Harley gritted her teeth and snatched the bottle before she could retort with something rude. "We'll see about that."

She stomped back to her desk.

"Everything all right?" asked Cosmo.

"Let's get this finished," Harley said. The smug look on Fenelda's face made her even more determined that their design would be a success.

At the end of the lesson, Professor Spark gathered them round to view the class's creations. Excited fizzles bounced quietly inside of Harley as she surveyed the prototypes.

Fenelda and Letti's looked neat with large paddles on the wheel, but it was too similar to what already existed so not very original. Dolores and Tarak's was impressive, with some sort of enhancing wind blades, but it wasn't

finished by a long way, so they probably wouldn't
win. Rufus and Henry's was a bit of a mess and
looked like they had tried a bit of every material
in the cupboard to make their wheel. Harley felt
certain that theirs was the strongest.

"Excellent work, Fenelda and Letti," said Professor Spark. "An interesting design to maximize the turbine." She approached the next pair. "Hmm, the structure looks a little weak, perhaps try a different material next time, but a solid effort." Next it was Harley and Cosmo's turn. "What a wonderful design. What is the funnel for?"

"We're using liquid light for a power boost," Harley said proudly. She could tell Professor Spark was impressed. Maybe the first step towards Pupil of the Term was in the bag.

Harley unstopped the bottle and tipped a little inside. There was a brief pause and then, with an almighty BOOM and an eruption of smoke and flashes, their mill caught fire.

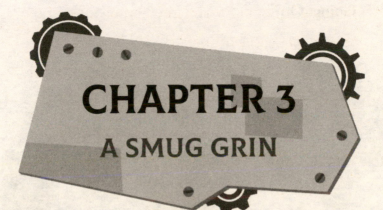

CHAPTER 3
A SMUG GRIN

The smoke alarm wailed and Professor Spark grabbed the fire extinguisher. In a moment the flames were out, leaving a mush of foam, charred metal and wood on the table. Harley stared in disbelief. How had this happened? It should have worked perfectly.

After thirty seconds of the class staring in stunned silence as Professor Spark turned the alarm off, Professor Fretshaw burst into the classroom. "What. In. All. Of. Inventia. Is. Going. On?"

Panic rose in an uncomfortable wave in Harley's throat. Professor Fretshaw must have heard the alarm and run from her office. This did not look good. How could it all be going so wrong on her first day? "Err, maybe it was a faulty component, I should have checked—"

"Harley Hitch," Professor Fretshaw snarled. "I might've known you'd be behind all this."

Harley put a hand to her cheek and wiped away a thick layer of soot.

"Professor Spark, I'll let you decide on a suitable punishment," said the head teacher, glaring.

Professor Spark passed Harley a star-speckled handkerchief for the soot. "I'm sure it was a mistake. No need for a punishment on the first day of term."

Professor Fretshaw tapped her foot

impatiently. "We must set the standards we wish to see for the rest of the term. Don't you agree, Professor Spark? Detention, at the very least."

Professor Spark gave a nod. "Very well. Harley and Cosmo, stay behind at the end of the lesson, please. Now, to announce the winners, whose design will be presented to Forgetown Electrical Company. Although your idea was indeed the most creative and well put together, Harley and Cosmo, on account of the mishap I have no choice but to disqualify you. Which means our winners are … Fenelda and Lettice. Congratulations, girls! Class is dismissed."

Harley felt as though the morning had been like watching her hopes and dreams spiral down a drain before she'd had a chance to even get started.

As the students bustled out of the classroom, Harley glanced at Cosmo. He was glaring at her from under his fringe.

"What? It wasn't my fault," Harley said, picking up the bottle of liquid light that had blown to the floor in the explosion. A cold wave of realization spread through her when she spotted the label. It wasn't liquid light, it was liquid fire!

"Are you sure about that?" Cosmo said under his breath, when he saw what she was looking at.

Harley's lips tightened, and for the second time that morning she felt her anger flare. "Well, maybe you should've checked it properly."

"It was your idea to use it; I would have thought you'd know what it looks like," he said quietly.

The last of the pupils to leave was Fenelda Spiggot, who lingered just long enough to flash Harley a smug grin. With a jolt, Harley remembered Fenelda had been the one to pass her the liquid light. She'd been set up.

"You'll need help with this mess," said Professor Fretshaw. She pressed a button on her digi-watch and a few seconds later a small tidy-bot rolled into the classroom. Tidy-bots were simple robots, spherical with lots of compartments and hands that popped out to sweep, polish and clean. "You took your time!" Professor Fretshaw snapped, before leaving the room. The tidy-bot let out an apologetic bleep.

"Now, what happened?" asked Professor Spark, turning to face Harley and Cosmo.

Harley showed her the liquid fire. Should she tell Professor Spark what she suspected?

But then, she had no proof. Just wait until she got her hands on that awful Fenelda. "I must have picked up the wrong bottle," she said in a small voice.

"Harley, you know the laboratory rules of always checking your equipment twice."

Harley nodded. Why hadn't she checked it before she used it? It was just like Fenelda to distract her on purpose and give her the wrong bottle. She should have guessed sooner.

"What's done is done. But detention might help remind you to be more vigilant in the future."

Harley couldn't believe she'd ended up with detention on her first day. She imagined the look on her grandparents' faces when she explained why she was home late. Beside her, Cosmo gulped loudly.

"Perhaps this can be a task that will also make it up to me a little." Professor Spark paused. "I'm in need of cogs for some small generators I'm building. I'd like you both to go to the Iron Forest after school and collect some for me. I need as many five-millimetre specimens as you can find. Do you have measuring tools?"

Harley nodded.

"Excellent."

Professor Spark went back to her desk. Harley glared at Cosmo. He could have checked too. She turned her glare into a scowl, although she was pretty sure he missed it, as he was hiding behind his long curly fringe.

Professor Spark picked up her electro-pad. "I'll write a note to your guardians now to inform them that you'll be late home. If you go straight after school, it shouldn't take you more than an hour. Bring the cogs in the morning. Now, hurry along to your next lesson."

Harley and Cosmo left the room, their heads and shoulders drooping.

"And try not to be late tomorrow," Professor Spark called after them.

CHAPTER 4
THE IRON FOREST

After a quiet afternoon of metal-craft with Professor Twine and Horticultural Studies with Professor Horatio, the Cogworks clock struck three and Harley met Cosmo outside to go to the Iron Forest. He was looking down and scuffing the ground with his foot. She wasn't looking forward to spending more time together. She'd only known him a day, but so far being around him had only meant trouble.

Sprocket was waiting at the gate with a few other robot pets who liked to meet their children. Rufus had a budgie-bot called Awk, and Lettice had a friendly rabbit robot called Coppertail, while Fenelda had a standard every-help-bot, which Harley didn't think had a name.

"Where are my snacks?" Fenelda snapped as she breezed up to it. "I told you to bring iced buns with jam. What are these? They look disgusting!"

"I am sorry, Miss Spiggot," said the bot. "We were out of jam so I thought oat bakes would—"

Fenelda stomped off.

Harley ran over to Sprocket, who jumped into her arms. "I missed you, wonder pup!" she said.

Cosmo sidled over. "He's got very springy legs," he said awkwardly.

Harley nodded curtly, and started down the path towards the Iron Forest. "Come on."

Cosmo's shoulders drooped as he walked. "My parents are going to be so cross. Who gets detention on their first day?"

"Maybe Professor Spark won't call it detention. She's kinder than Professor Fretshaw. She might just say we're helping her with a task." Harley hoped so. She didn't think she could bear to see Grandpa Elliot's disappointed expression or Grandpa Eden's sympathetic shrug when they learned she'd already been in trouble.

Cosmo shuffled his feet unhappily.

"Look, the sooner we get this done, the sooner we can get home and find out."

They carried on in awkward silence, until it became so awkward that Harley begrudgingly felt she had to fill it. "Things must seem different here to the city."

Cosmo nodded. "It's quieter … well, in some ways." He glanced at her, as though wondering whether she might set off another explosion.

"Why did you move to Forgetown?"

"Mum's work. She's overseeing the Forgetown officials, something about bringing processes in line with the city."

"That sounds … important." She wanted to say boring but resisted. "Do you miss your friends?"

Cosmo shrugged. "I suppose." His cheeks blushed red.

"Well, I think friends are more trouble than they're worth," said Harley, feeling another surge of anger at Fenelda.

"Right." He paused. "I've been meaning to visit the Iron Forest since we arrived, but we've been busy unpacking and I didn't want to go on my own."

"Why ever not?" Harley loved living so close to the Iron Forest. If she needed a part for an invention, or if Grandpa Elliot needed a new mechanism for the printing press, they would come here with a picnic and make a day of it. Once they'd found a fully formed plough growing deep in the forest, which had proved very useful for Grandpa Eden in the garden. The whole of Inventia used the Iron Forest for mechanical supplies and robot parts; there was plenty for all, although people were careful to not take more than was naturally replenished.

"Well, it might be a bit spooky."

"It's really not scary, it's magical."

Cosmo didn't look convinced. "I read about it in Inventia City Library. I've visited Forgetown Library already, of course. It's small but seems well stocked."

Harley shrugged. She preferred to spend her time outside rather than in a room full of dusty books.

As they turned a corner, late afternoon sunbeams hit the forest, making it glimmer like an emerald-and-silver jewel box in the valley of Forgetown. Trees of various shapes and sizes zigzagged across the sky, a fusion of natural green and metallic growth. Harley felt as though the warmth of the sunlight shone inside of her too. Not for the first time, she was reminded how lucky she was to live so near it. As detentions went, maybe this wasn't so bad.

Cosmo stopped. "Wow, that's impressive. Better than the pictures in the books. Isn't it amazing to think that spare parts actually grow there?"

Harley nodded. "Wait until you see inside."

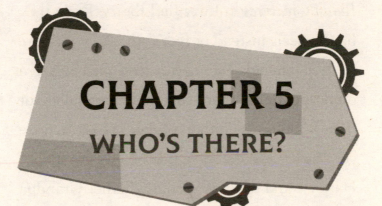

CHAPTER 5
WHO'S THERE?

As they walked down the path towards the Iron Forest, Harley told Cosmo some more about it. "It can be quite random, but there are some great staples, like the cogweed, nailberry bushes and needle pines. It's the most marvellous place. Grandpa Elliot says we should never take it for granted. Do you know there are creatures that you can only find in the Iron Forest, like the velocipede?"

"I saw a picture of one once in a book called *Rarest Creatures* in Inventia Library. Don't they have wheels instead of feet?"

"Yes, though I've never seen one. They're extremely shy so there isn't much known about them – although Grandpa Eden swears he once got a ride home on one when he was at school!" Harley could never work out whether Grandpa Eden was joking about this, but she enjoyed picturing it and liked to think it might be true.

They entered the forest. Harley loved the gentle sounds here: the wind through the trees, the birdsong and the occasional snuffle of ironhogs.

"If we see one of these velocipedes we should be careful. It might seem shy, but you said yourself that not much is known about them," said Cosmo, looking around anxiously.

"Cosmo, they're peaceful."

"If you've never seen one in real life you don't know that."

Harley tried not to roll her eyes. Cosmo was obviously a bit of a worrier. "Let's focus on the cogs, shall we? Remember, five millimetres only. I have a ruler," she said, pulling one from her belt.

"And I have gloves."

"Why?" said Harley with a frown. "It's not that cold."

"Extra-thick gardening gloves," he said. "You don't want to cut yourself."

Harley had never brought gardening gloves

to the forest. She liked to feel nature and didn't care about getting dirty hands or the odd scratch.

Sprocket suddenly leaped ahead and barked.

"He's found some!" said Harley, hurrying over to a patch of plants with fronds unfurling and various cogs growing on the ends. "Good boy, Sprocket. Let's get picking."

Cosmo hurried over and started examining the plant. He beamed. "Wow, it's so cool to see one in real life! We need to find younger plants that will more likely be growing five-millimetre cogs. They'll be nearer the ground."

Harley looked up, surprised. "Do you know a lot about plants, then?" She hadn't really taken Cosmo for an outdoorsy type, with his neatly pressed uniform and pristine white shirt.

Cosmo's eyes lit up. "Plants are the best!" he said.

"Oh-kaaay! That was a little more enthusiastic than I'd expected. You should meet my grandpa Eden."

"Does he love plants too? Has he been to Inventia Botanic Gardens? It's amazing. There are samples from distant Mezalia and the Zinctile plains."

This was the most sparky Harley had seen Cosmo since she'd met him. His cheeks glowed with enthusiasm. It was nice. Perhaps he wasn't so bad after all. He was right, she should have read the label before she'd used the liquid fire. It was silly to be frosty with him, especially as he seemed to have forgotten now that he'd been cross with her too.

"What do you like best, Harley?"

She thought for a moment. "I guess I like stars most. There's a star-chatter observatory in town which is the most magical place. One day I'd like to be an astronaut and go to space. Well, after I've invented a space transport."

They began collecting the cogs, losing themselves in the quiet rhythm. After a while, a strange growl interrupted the silence.

Cosmo's head whipped up and he looked around in fright.

Harley grinned. "Don't worry. That was just my stomach groaning for food."

A metal hatch flipped open in Sprocket's back and a cupcake appeared.

"Sprocket, you're a genius!" Harley glanced at Cosmo, then she broke it in two and passed half to him.

"Thanks." Cosmo beamed. "He's a cool dog."

"I adapted him with my grandpas. At first, he didn't do much, but we're always adding something new – a radar, tail transmitter, turbo legs, that sort of thing. One day I'd like to make him a voice transmitter, but it's quite tricky technology."

They fell silent as they both munched on their halves of the cupcake.

After a moment Harley said, "I'm sorry I got you into trouble. I should've checked the bottle of liquid light."

"I should've checked it too."

Harley stared at Cosmo. "Did you see Fenelda's face?"

"The girl with the immaculate hair?"

"That's her. I think she distracted me in the store cupboard and passed me the wrong bottle. Liquid fire looks very similar to liquid light."

Cosmo looked disbelieving. "Why would she do that?"

"Fenelda doesn't want anyone else to win Pupil of the Term. She likes to be the best. Didn't you see that golden light bulb pinned to her chest? The thing she can't stop touching? I've always been her main competition and she hates that.

"Professor Fretshaw makes it obvious Fenelda's her favourite. Last year it didn't matter how well I did in any assignment, it was always Fenelda this and Fenelda that, so I kind of thought, what's the use of trying?"

"You gave up?"

Harley shrugged. When she'd been blamed for every little mishap, it had been easy to fall behind and get into more trouble. This year, in Professor Spark's class, she was determined for things to be different. "Come on, let's get the last few; it's getting late."

Shuffling sounded not far away. Harley looked up. "Sprocket?" She hoped he wasn't eating the oil pods again. It had taken a whole day to clean out his nostrils last time.

Sprocket nudged her ankle. "Oh, you're here!" she said. She strained to see into the thicket where the noise had come from. All was quiet now.

"What's the matter?" Cosmo asked, his eyes larger than lily pads.

"Nothing. Maybe it was an ironhog snouting around."

"An ironhog?" said Cosmo nervously.

"Don't worry, they're perfectly harmless

– part metal, part organic. They're only interested in tool truffles."

A tall shadow moved through the trees. "Who's there?" Harley called, her heart thudding against the front of her chest. Grandpa Eden had once told her about a silver bear, king of the Iron Forest, who legend said visited during the full moon. Of course, it was a just a story and it wasn't a full moon. Or was it?

The shape became very still. Harley squinted into the gloom. It was about the height of a person; with a bolt she knew exactly what it was, or more precisely who it was. Fenelda.

Harley stood up indignantly. "Fenelda Spiggot! If it wasn't enough wrecking our assignment today, you have to follow us into the forest to … well, to do whatever you're planning

next. Probably stealing all the cogs that we collected so we get into even more trouble." She beckoned Cosmo.

He glared, wide-eyed. A shaking hand tucked some hair behind his ear.

Harley whispered, "When I go, follow me." She looked down at Sprocket. "Go for her ankles." Harley rolled up her sleeves. "One, two … Agggghhh!" And she charged towards the shape.

But as they ran, Cosmo lost his footing, yelped, and flew forward. Something splattered into the air like an explosion of dark fireworks, landing with a thick scatter of squelches, and covering Harley and Sprocket. Cosmo lay face down in a patch of oil pods.

"Oh, great!" Harley said, looking at her uniform, which now had great gungy black patches smattered over her waistcoat, shirt and skirt as though she'd been shot with a paint gun. Grandpa Eden wouldn't be so bothered about the mess; he was always covered in soil from gardening himself, but Grandpa Elliot had taken a lot of time to press her uniform the night before. She'd so wanted to give them a reason to smile when she would tell them about her first day back. She glanced back into the trees to see that Fenelda had gone, and let her hands flop angrily to her sides. She'd take it up with her tomorrow at school.

Sprocket sprang happily into the air, then rotated on his back, spreading the oil even further. Harley rolled her eyes and looked to Cosmo, who was pushing himself up from the patch. His face was covered in shiny, gooey black oil, just two white eyes blinking in shock.

"Are you all right?" she said, her anger at Fenelda melting away at the funny sight of a very gloopy Cosmo.

"I just wanted to get through today without anything rotten happening," he said. Then he smiled, and Sprocket let out a series of fast bleeps that sounded like a laugh, and Harley couldn't help laughing too.

"Look at the state of us!" she said, trying to flick off some of the oil, which stubbornly clung to her hand.

After a while Cosmo wrinkled his nose and said, "My parents will go mad. Mum's always nagging me to tuck my shirt in, so she's not going to like this one bit."

"Probably not." Harley smiled sympathetically.

"Come on, we've got enough cogs to keep Professor Spark happy. Let's go back to my house. Grandpa Eden will be able to help. We'll cut through the forest."

"What if we get lost?"

"You worry an awful lot, Cosmo."

Sprocket's tail extended skyward, turned, and flashed red.

"Sprocket has an inbuilt homing device, and I've known the forest all my life. Getting lost is impossible!"

They hadn't gone far before something caught Harley's eye. She stopped and peered at what appeared to be a fungus growing on one of the trees. It was a peculiar, many-layered pattern of umbrella shapes that seemed to ripple with indigo, ruby, lime, orange and blue. "I've never seen anything like this growing here."

They crouched down to look.

"Wow! What is it?" asked Cosmo.

"I'm not sure." She leaned in to look closer. The rainbow colours reflected off her oily clothes.

Cosmo shook his head. "The changing colours are unusual. And … it might be the ripples of light, but it seems to be moving."

Harley looked up at the trunk of the tree. It could be an exciting new plant to investigate. The shiny gold light bulb danced in her mind. "Come on. Let's get back and get cleaned up. We can ask Grandpa Eden."

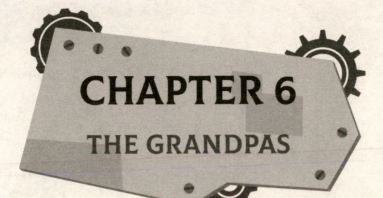

CHAPTER 6
THE GRANDPAS

Hitch House was a beautiful hotchpotch of styles and makeshift parts, as though several houses had donated parts of themselves to be brought together to create one whole that somehow worked. Harley thought it was the best home in all of Forgetown, not only because it was unique, but because it was full of happy memories: like painting the star constellations on her bedroom alongside Grandpa Eden;

baking walnut bread with Grandpa Elliot in their cosy kitchen; and making the staircase into a slide and shooting down it with Sprocket.

"We're going to be so late, much more than an hour," said Cosmo with a huff.

But Harley was thinking about the strange fungus again. Might this new discovery make up for everything that had happened today and even be her ticket to Pupil of the Term?

"I'm going to start calling you Cosmo Worry Pants. Look, it won't take too long to get cleaned up. Then you can go home and your parents will never know about the oil pods."

He looked at her doubtfully.

"Come on, Grandpa Eden is in the greenhouse."

Grandpa Eden was tending his large patch of strawberry plants. He looked up. "What in Forgetown happened to you?"

"We stumbled into an oil pod patch."

"No kidding!" He stroked his peppery-grey beard. Harley thought he had the kindest blue eyes she'd ever seen, and his cheeks were always rosy. He was an outdoorsy free spirit who was often found getting messy in the garden, and he was usually more understanding of her mishaps than Grandpa Elliot.

"Do you have any of that stuff you used to help me clean up Sprocket last time?"

"The oil diffuser leaves? Yes, I cultivated several more plants after Sprocket took a liking to the pods, just in case. I didn't expect to be using them on you!" He laughed. "And your friend here?"

"This is Cosmo. It was his first day. He's just moved from the city."

"The big house on Hinge Street? I think I

saw you moving in when I popped into town for supplies. Welcome!"

"Thank you." Cosmo looked around the greenhouse in wonder. "Wow, there's so much in here! And you have strawberries growing in September!"

Grandpa Eden nodded proudly. "It's all down to our indoor mechani-weather robot."

A robot walked out from behind a large palm. She was a little taller than Grandpa Eden, with human-looking limbs.

"She's called Daisy and is Grandpa Eden's finest garden invention. He adapted her from an every-help-bot. He's making more for the Horticultural Society too."

The robot put a metal finger to the pot of a nearby cucumber plant.

Grandpa patted the robot on the back. "She's fitted with over fifty sensors and probes so that she can detect which plants need which weather at any time. Right now, she's checking the soil moisture levels."

"Incredible," said Cosmo.

"If the weather gets too cold, she can shine like the sun. Daisy, would you mind showing the young man, please?"

In an instant, Daisy's face glowed golden orange, casting a warm light over the cucumber plant. Then her hand flipped back and a sprinkler spout watered the plant.

"Wow!"

"Her chest can hold over a hundred litres, and she pops outside to fill up when it's raining. Very economical. Now, come on, you two, let's sort that oil out," said Grandpa Eden, leading them towards a large pot plant bursting with feathery white flowered plants. He plucked a couple of the flowers and handed one to each of them. Harley brushed her arm with the flower and it began absorbing the oil like magic.

"Incredible!" said Cosmo. "I've never seen anything like it. That's two new plants in one day."

"What else have you seen?" asked Grandpa Eden.

"The strangest thing was growing in the Iron Forest," said Harley excitedly. She couldn't wait to hear what he thought. She leaned in. "It changed colour."

"We think it was some sort of fungus," said Cosmo.

Grandpa Eden frowned. "Colour changing,

you say?"

They nodded.

"Odd, very odd," he said thoughtfully.

Grandpa Eden took a book from one of his greenhouse shelves. He flicked through the pages and shrugged. "Perhaps a new strain of fungus has blown in from beyond the borders."

Harley hovered at his side. "It could be a new discovery! Maybe we'd be famous and it would be named after us!" She felt a warm glow as she imagined being on the stage at Cogworks, Fenelda Spiggot begrudgingly handing over her golden light bulb badge and Professor Fretshaw looking at her proudly for once.

"You want to have a fungus named after you?" asked Cosmo, hiding a small smile.

"Enough dreaming of glory, Harley," said Grandpa Eden. "Why don't you tell your professor first thing in the morning? For now, let's get you two cleaned up."

"Ah, there you are! Late for dinner again." Grandpa Elliot popped his head around the greenhouse door.

He wore his neat tweed work suit with his favourite pocket digi-watch, which always kept him on time. His grey hair and white beard were much tidier than Grandpa Eden's. "Oh, we have a guest. Will you be joining us too?"

"Thank you, but I can't stay. My mum and dad will be cross enough about the detention, so I should get home."

"Detention?" said both grandpas, looking at Harley.

"Ah … there was a small accident with liquid fire that absolutely wasn't our fault—"

Grandpa Elliot put a hand up to quieten Harley. "We had a message from Professor Spark to say you would be late because she'd set you a task." He exchanged a frown with Grandpa Eden.

Harley flashed an apologetic smile. "I'm sorry, Grandpa."

"Perhaps you can tell us everything over dinner," said Grandpa Eden. "Meanwhile, you and I will give Cosmo a lift home."

Grandpa Elliot gave a nod and went back to the house.

They finished clearing up the oil, and Grandpa Eden drove Cosmo and Harley to Cosmo's house in his tri-wheel trundle bike.

They rattled up the lane towards a pristine house. "Wow, your house is huge," said Harley.

Cosmo's mum opened the door. "There you are. I was getting worried. Professor Spark said she'd asked you to collect something in the forest for her?"

Cosmo glanced at Grandpa Eden and Harley. "Err … yes."

"How very helpful of you. I'm glad to hear you're working hard on your first day, Cosmo," said Mrs Willoughby.

"This is Harley, and I'm her grandpa Eden. Welcome to Forgetown," he said, handing Cosmo's mum one of his extra-large prize marrows. He smiled as she took the marrow and held it as though it was from another planet.

"Err … lovely," she said, then pressed a button on her watch.

A small robot zoomed up the hallway behind her. "Every-HELP-bot at your service."

"Take this to the kitchen." She handed the marrow to the robot.

"Yes, Mrs Willoughby."

"Come along inside, Cosmo," said Mrs Willoughby.

"We'd better get going, our dinner is waiting. It was lovely to meet you, Cosmo, Mrs Willoughby." Grandpa Eden nodded politely.

Mrs Willoughby disappeared inside without another word.

Cosmo was about to follow her when Harley pulled on his arm. "We should take the cogs to Professor Spark before school and tell her about the fungus."

He shuffled his feet. "I'd rather just you do it."

Something inside Harley twisted a little at his words. She hadn't realized it until that moment, but they'd got on well in the Iron Forest and perhaps they had started to become friends, in spite of their shaky start. But she nodded. He was right. It was probably best they stayed away from each other if the first day was anything to go by. "I guess I'll see you in class, then," she said, following Grandpa Eden back to the trundle bike.

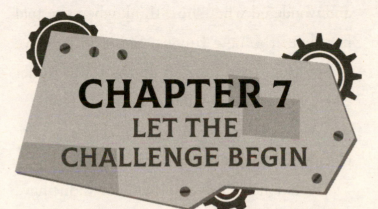

CHAPTER 7
LET THE
CHALLENGE BEGIN

Next morning, Harley hurried into school with the basket of cogs.

"Harley Hitch," declared Primbot. "Eight thirty ... my readings must be malfunctioning. You're ... early!"

"Yes, I am, smarty-pants."

"I'm going to get my components checked," Primbot muttered.

Harley smiled to herself as she thought how

pleased Professor Spark would be with the cogs and wondered what she'd think when she told her about the new fungus. She said goodbye to Sprocket, then hurried up the tower to her classroom, where she found Professor Spark.

"We collected your cogs," Harley said, placing the basket on the table.

"Well done. They're perfect. You didn't have to come in early to give them to me, although I am pleased you're not late. Is Cosmo with you?" She glanced over Harley's shoulder.

Harley shook her head, and felt a surprising pang. They'd had fun in the end. She was sorry he didn't want to be friends. "He did help, but I wanted to come in early so I said I would bring them to you." After a pause she said, "There's something else I need to tell you." She explained about the strange new fungus, watching Professor Spark's face carefully for a reaction. Would she be impressed? "I think we might have discovered a new type! It could be fun to investigate."

"It does sound curious and different." Professor Spark tapped a star-topped pencil on the table. "This could be an excellent learning opportunity. I say we scrap the planned lesson and go on a class expedition to take a look. What do you think?"

Harley nodded keenly, liking Professor Spark more and more.

The class gradually arrived. When Cosmo walked through the door they gave each other a stiff nod and sat beside each other in silence. Professor Spark explained the morning's mission and the class set off.

Cosmo walked at the back while Harley

made sure she was close to Fenelda as they made their way down the path towards the Iron Forest. She stepped beside her. "I know you gave me the liquid fire, and I know you were spying on us yesterday after school."

"Don't be ridiculous. And spying? On you? I've got far better ways to spend my time." Fenelda laughed airily.

Harley squinted disbelievingly.

"Or perhaps you're right. Yes, that's it, I was trying to spy on your latest hairstyle. What creation would you call it today? Two currant buns?"

"Funny." Harley scowled. She was wearing two bunches high up on either side of her head which she'd twisted into domes and pinned. Harley thought it was different and cool.

Fenelda walked on with her nose in the air.

"I expect this expedition is all a waste of time and you've just made up the fungus to get more attention."

Harley pulled her shoulders back and held her head high as she moved past to talk to Letti. She hadn't expected Fenelda to confess. Experience had taught her that Fenelda was good at acting innocent, but at least now she knew that Harley was on to her.

When they reached the area where she and Cosmo had seen the fungus, Harley stopped in amazement. She counted quickly. Ten trees were now covered with the neon, rippling fungus. Not only that, the leaves of the trees were now ash white and the branches drooped unhappily, as though the fungus had taken all of their life force. She hadn't noticed it yesterday. The surrounding cogberries had shrivelled up too.

"It was only on one tree before," Harley said, puzzled.

"Nobody touch a thing," said Professor Spark forcefully. The class froze. "Are you certain, Harley? Perhaps you didn't notice it on the other trees?" She frowned. "No fungus spreads that quickly."

"I'm certain," said Harley. She'd never seen anything like it. Not even Grandpa Eden's strawberries grew this fast after a dose of his super grow formula. She didn't know much about fungus, but she knew this wasn't normal. She stared at the dead plants at her feet. If it was spreading so quickly, what would this mean for the beautiful forest? She couldn't bear the thought of it being harmed, and it would be disastrous for Forgetown and Inventia if machinery supplies ran out. Inventions were the heart of their town. How would people make anything new, or repair machines? The last time Dr Orbit's anti-gravity machine had broken, it took months for the forest to grow enough parts, and Miss Li had told Harley her robot postal pigeons got through a whole plant of wing brackets most weeks.

"It could be a new type of fungus with aggressive traits," said Professor Spark, worry lines creasing her forehead. "I'll take a sample back to school. Professor Horatio will need to see it, and we should report this to the Horticultural Society of Forgetown immediately."

Harley could tell by the serious tone of Professor Spark's voice that she was as concerned as Harley was.

Professor Spark took some gloves from her bag and a tool from her belt. "Everybody stay where you are and do not touch it." She carefully scraped a sample from the tree and put it into a jar. She sealed the lid tightly. "This could be incredibly hazardous," she said, almost to herself.

Then Professor Spark declared that they

should return to school.

As the class began walking back to the path outside the Iron Forest, Harley paused, thoughts bouncing around her mind. OK, this was bad. But maybe she could help. Perhaps there was an opportunity here that could play to her strengths.

Cosmo, who had stayed away from her up until now, hung back. "Are you all right?" he asked shyly.

She nodded, but her mind was whirring.

"What are you thinking?" he asked.

She hesitated, then decided to tell him. "OK. I'm thinking that this is a problem."

Cosmo squinted. "Yes?"

She raised her eyebrows. "Think about it, Cosmo. What would happen if the fungus completely overtook the Iron Forest? Some of the trees are hundreds of years old, and many species of plants here are unique to the forest. It would be terrible. And it would be disastrous for Forgetown and Inventia; no spare parts, nothing new would get invented. Mr Bobbins at Cosmic Sewing makes all the uniforms for Cogworks, he even exports to Inventia; he'd never keep up without his fleet of mechanical sewing hands. He needs a regular supply of needles and pins from the forest. And the oil sap from the needle pines is essential for greasing the joints of machines like Grandpa Elliot's rocket-propelled bicycle. We need to do something."

And if Harley solved the problem, maybe… Well, maybe Pupil of the Term wouldn't be completely out of the question after all.

"What are you two whispering about?"

Fenelda peered from behind a tree.

Harley felt a surge of annoyance. "Nel Spiggot, you're more slippery than an oil pod. How long have you been there?"

"Long enough. And I bet you think you can find the answer to this?" Fenelda laughed.

"Yes, and why not?"

"After the trouble you caused yesterday, you should probably leave it to the experts." She flicked her black bob.

Harley huffed and blew a stray bit of hair away from her lips. "You're right. I'm sure the professors will solve it. Forget you heard a thing."

Fenelda leaned in. "I mean, *you* should leave it to the experts." She gestured to herself. "The person who could solve this would have a free ticket to Cogworks Pupil of the Term."

"I was actually thinking about the forest," Harley said, narrowing her eyes, though the sun glinted on Fenelda's golden light bulb badge and she felt a jealous burn in her chest.

Cosmo shuffled from one foot to the other. Fenelda fixed him with her gaze. "You should choose better friends, Cosmo. Harley Hitch is a disaster waiting to happen. You'd do better to find someone else, if you want to fit in here."

"I'm not, we're not … friends. I just don't want anyone to get into trouble," said Cosmo, looking down. His glasses slipped to the ground and he hurriedly retrieved them.

Harley narrowed her eyes at Fenelda. "Do you think you could come up with a solution for the fungus quicker than me?"

"I know I can."

Cosmo looked between them nervously.

"Then let the challenge begin," said Fenelda, skipping away.

CHAPTER 8

RUSTY RIVER

"I've got to find a way to solve this before Fenelda does," said Harley.

Cosmo frowned. "You should stay out of it. It's pretty serious."

Harley put a hand up. "Fenelda will be looking for a way, and I'm not going to let her beat me again." She couldn't bear the thought of the forest being in danger, but the thought of Fenelda being the one to save the day was even worse.

"But—"

"I'll go to Rusty River after school. For inspiration"

"Rusty River?"

"Yes, that's what I said. I'm going fishing."

Cosmo looked at her as though she was a curious specimen. "What are you up to? I don't think that'll solve anything."

"For someone who doesn't want to be friends – and the feeling is mutual, by the way – you seem very interested in what I'm up to."

"I just don't like trouble, and you should be careful after yesterday."

"Cosmo, it's fishing. It helps you think." The Rusty River was a place that had helped her many times before.

"Really?" he said doubtfully. "Because I have a heap of books back home and they're probably more useful than fishing. I really think you should leave the fungus problem to the officials."

Harley pulled what appeared to be a miniature version of Sprocket out of her waistcoat pocket.

"What's that?" he asked.

"It's my Pocket Sprocket: I speak to it and a signal transmits to Sprocket at home." She held it in her palm and pressed the nose, which lit green. "Sprocket, could you bring a fishing rod with you after school, please?"

The tiny model Sprocket let out a mechanical bark.

"Thanks, buddy." She depressed the nose and put it back in her pocket.

Cosmo shook his head and hurried to catch up with the others.

*

Later, Sprocket bounded up the lane with a fishing rod in his mouth. He greeted Harley and the two of them hurried to the mill at Rusty River. It wasn't clear what Harley could do to stop the fungus, but she couldn't just sit around and do nothing. If it had caused so much damage in one night, who knew how much more the fungus had spread by now? She hoped the Rusty River would set her in the right direction. It had in the past, like the time she'd been trying to work out how to get mechani-wings to work and it had given her just the piece of information she was looking for. At least Fenelda wouldn't be here; she'd always said the Rusty River was a lot of gobbledegook and nonsense.

On the way, Harley saw some figures further along the valley. She pulled a telescopic viewer from a pocket; they were Forgetown officials dressed in their fog-grey jackets with two rows of large brass buttons down the chest. They were holding some tape and rope and were heading towards the Iron Forest. Then hushed footsteps nearby caught Harley's attention, but she acted as though she hadn't heard. She glanced at Sprocket and put a finger to her lips. Then, quick as an electric pulse, she turned and leaped to where the sound had come from. "Nel! Oh…" She frowned and pulled Cosmo from the bushes. "What are you doing?"

"I was checking on what you were up to." Cosmo looked defensive. He gestured to the officials in the distance. "See, there's no need to interfere. They've got it all in hand."

Harley stuffed her viewer back in its pocket. "But what if they can't find a solution before the fungus gets out of control? Grandpa Elliot says they have so many paperwork hoops to jump through there should be prizes awarded when someone actually does something." Plus, she felt responsible; after all, she'd discovered the fungus. She huffed past Cosmo and carried on towards the river.

Soon she reached the mill, which turned slowly as the red-brown river flowed past. The afternoon sun caught the great brass-and-wood wheel paddles in regular flashes of light.

Cosmo appeared beside her and scratched his head through his layers of curls. "What is this place? That water doesn't look very clean. I don't think you'll catch any fish in it."

Harley was surprised to see that Cosmo had followed her. She had never brought anyone with her to Rusty River before, apart from Sprocket. Not that she'd brought Cosmo. She knew he was only tagging along to make sure she didn't accidentally explode something, but still, part of her was excited to show him what the river could do. "You'll have to wait and see." She smiled.

She sat on the bridge, legs dangling down.

Cosmo perched on a rock close by. "Don't you need some bait or something?"

"Not for these fish." Harley cast her line into the water.

"I don't see what this will do. I know you said fishing helps you think, but wouldn't you be better off going to the library or researching on the InventiaNet?"

Harley ignored him. Books worked for some people, but Grandpa Eden always said that the best answers were out in the wild, if you knew the right places to look and listen, and Harley agreed.

After a while, Cosmo said, "The river isn't actually rusty, is it?"

Harley shook her head. "It's the minerals from the copper mountain that give the

colour. Now, shush; I need to concentrate…
Come on, come on," she repeated under her
breath. After a while, her line tensed. "I've
got one!" Swiftly, she yanked her rod back
and a great metal trout flew from the water.

She reeled it in, unhooked the line, and grasped it so that its face was towards her. "I'm ready, tell me," she said, staring eagerly into its glassy eyes.

Cosmo coughed. "Are you all right? I mean, it's a metal fish."

The trout threw him a glare.

"Yes, I know," Harley said impatiently. "This is the only place they live, and we're fishing for inspiration, I told you. We catch a fish, it gives us advice, and we work out the answer to the fungus problem."

The trout looked back at Harley, cleared its throat in an over-the-top way, paused, then said, "Patience is a bitter plant, but the fruit is sweet."

Harley hurled the trout back into the river. How could patience possibly help? "I'm going to try again." She recast her line.

"Harley," said Cosmo, folding his arms. "That can't be the way it's supposed to work. You're not meant to ignore advice until you hear something you like."

"Shh, I've got another one." Harley reeled in the next fish: a small metal mackerel this time. She quickly unhooked it. "This is the one, Cosmo. I can feel it." Harley thought back to the end of last year when she'd watched Fenelda take Pupil of the Term for the third time and she'd been so upset that she hadn't wanted to go home after school. She had come here. A fish had told her not to be afraid of growing slowly, but to be afraid of standing still, and she knew it meant she had to keep trying.

The mackerel cleared its throat elaborately. "The answer you seek is—"

Suddenly, a huge pike leaped out of the water and swallowed the mackerel whole.

Harley yelped. "No! That was the one! I can't believe it! It was about to tell me the answer, then that bigger fish had to come and ruin it! The nerve, the cheek, the…"

She stared wide-eyed at Cosmo. An excited fizzle had ignited inside her chest. "Hold on a moment."

"What?"

"A bigger fish. I need a bigger fish." Could this be the answer? The idea was expanding like a slow-motion firework. Sprocket tilted his head and gave a curious yap.

"A bigger fish?" Cosmo said doubtfully.

"A predator! Think about it, Cosmo. One person's meat is another's poison; I heard that from a fish once. Anyway, all we need is a bigger fish that loves fungus!" The answer was almost with her, but not quite.

Cosmo wrinkled a nostril as though she was quite bonkers. "I don't think fish eat fungus."

"Not an actual fish, silly! Do any animals eat fungus, Cosmo?"

He thought for a moment. "I think so: badgers, deer, rabbits, mice … ooh, and squirrels. But that fungus is fierce, it might kill them."

Harley thought for a moment; he was right. "We need something tougher than the normal predator." For some reason, a conversation she'd had with Grandpa Eden over the summer popped into her head. He had a constant battle with slugs eating his strawberries and lettuces… She looked at Cosmo. "I've got the answer! It's slugs!"

"Slugs?" he said doubtfully.

"Yes! Grandpa Eden told me they've been around about one hundred and fifty million years, which is a lot longer than humans. He said they were – what was the word he used? – resilient!"

Cosmo's frown deepened. He took off his glasses and cleaned them with a hankie from his waistcoat pocket. "There's a book called *The Great Minibeast Compendium* and I'm sure I once read that slugs can eat poisonous mushrooms without getting sick."

"Then that's it! Slugs are the answer!"

"We should go to Forgetown Library after school tomorrow," said Cosmo. "There are bound to be more books on the subject there." He stopped, then said hastily, "I mean, you should go there. This is your idea."

"Hmm, maybe." But Harley didn't want to waste another day thinking and checking books.

"And you would need an awful lot of slugs," Cosmo said. "If that fungus is still spreading, a few slugs won't work."

Harley smiled. An addition to the idea was blossoming in her brain. "Not a few slugs. I have a plan. And if you insist on keeping an eye on me, you'll have to come to tea and see."

CHAPTER 9

SUPER GROW

"What's your big idea, Harley?" asked Cosmo as they hurried back to Hitch House.

"I'm going to borrow some of Grandpa Eden's super grow and use it on a slug."

Cosmo stared at her, wide-eyed.

"Don't you think it's the best idea you've ever heard?" she said excitedly. "I'd like to see snooty old Fenelda come up with something as good as this."

"Harley, I'm not sure. What if it doesn't work? You've already been in trouble once and—"

"—and that just means I…" She paused. If Cosmo was here, he might as well help. "We need to work doubly hard to solve this!"

"So, you're going to try to upsize a slug?"

She thought for a moment. Grandpa Eden made the super grow himself using a secret formula which he said only involved natural, organic ingredients. Surely that meant it would be perfectly safe for the slug? It would either work, or it would just be a delicious slug snack. "Super grow is for strawberries usually, but it's worth a try. If I make a slug, say, twice, maybe three times its usual size, it should be able to chomp through the fungus quickly."

Cosmo blinked behind his glasses and

shuffled his feet as though an ant was tickling his toes. She noticed he did this when he was feeling uncomfortable. Perhaps she was rushing things a bit, but there was no time to spare if she wanted to save the forest and beat Fenelda. And if he hated it so much, maybe she should tell him to go home? She worked best alone. But then … she had enjoyed going to the Iron Forest and the Rusty River together. It was nice feeling part of a team somehow.

"Cosmo, I think you've lived in the city for too long. You need to expand your sense of adventure. Come on!"

"OK. But just to make sure you don't get into trouble."

She rolled her eyes, then tugged his arm to continue walking along the path.

*

"Hello, Grandpas!" Harley called when they were close to the house. "Do you mind if Cosmo stays for tea?"

"Of course not," said Grandpa Elliot, poking his head out of the kitchen window. "You're just in time to set the table."

Tea was Grandpa Eden's many-vegetable casserole and super cheesy scones from Cog Mill Bakery.

"It was a busy afternoon at the paper," said Grandpa Elliot. "They want me to report on that fungus growing in the Iron Forest. They're already talking about restrictions on spare parts. So far today I've discovered that a quarter of the postal pigeons are offline, Kitchen Imagine has cancelled the launch of their new soup-cooling spoons and carrot-peeling machines, the Forgetown Square clockwork cuckoo is stuck singing 'Invention No.7 in E Minor', which is driving everyone round the bend, and the cog-shaping pasta machine at Picante's Pizza Parlour is broken. I guess none of them can get what they need."

Harley and Cosmo exchanged a look.

"It's spreading quickly," continued Grandpa Elliot. "Unlike anything they've seen. If it takes too much of a hold, who knows what it'll mean? Business closures, no parts even to mend the simplest problem. Eden, what will you do if your rotavator axle breaks again, if you can't go to the Iron Forest for a replacement?"

Grandpa Eden nodded with a frown. "How curious this fungus is. I'm glad you children reported it quickly. Make sure you stay away; it sounds dangerous. Let's hope the authorities find a solution, and quickly."

There was a look on Cosmo's face that made Harley think he felt compelled to tell them about her plan. His lips parted a little and Harley swiftly nudged his foot with hers under the table.

Grandpa Elliot offered the bread around. "I went down to the forest to see for myself. The Forgetown officials already have it cordoned off and the Horticultural Society has started investigating."

Grandpa Eden shook his head. "I hope they're quick. I've heard that they've tried digging it up and scraping it, but the action seems to release a high amount of spores, which means it comes back faster than they're removing it, and more aggressively. It could take days to find a solution, with all the procedure and paperwork. And apparently they're all arguing about the best thing to do."

After tea, Harley said they needed to work on an assignment upstairs. "We have to wait until it's getting dark for the slugs to come out," she whispered to Cosmo. She was even more eager to get started after what her grandpas had said.

"How about that weather-bot of yours, Daisy? Won't she say something if she sees us?"

"Grandpa Eden puts her on charge from teatime until after breakfast. Don't worry."

Later, as the sun began to set, they crept past the grandpas chatting in the lounge, and into Grandpa Eden's greenhouse. The hairs on Harley's arms tingled with anticipation.

Cosmo pulled Harley's arm. "How will we see them? It's too gloomy."

Sprocket's eyes flashed and became two beams of light.

Harley smiled proudly. "He's no ordinary dog!"

"I wish I had a robot pet."

"Why don't you make one? Or you could buy one from the robo-pet shop."

"I'm not allowed. Mum says robots are for duty, not for fun."

Harley frowned. She couldn't imagine not being able to play with Sprocket. "Well, you can hang out with Sprocket any time. He's really good at powerball. There's a mechanism that shoots balls from his mouth, and you have to catch them." She looked around. "OK, so we'll need to give the slug something it will love to eat, and then think of a safe way to stop it escaping until the morning."

"They love lettuce, or strawberries," said Cosmo.

"Good idea. Grandpa Eden grows loads of lettuces; he won't miss one." She took one from the patch. "Cosmo, grab a lettuce protector cage from over there. I'll get the super grow, then we're ready to find a slug."

Sprocket shone his torchlit eyes in different directions so that Harley and Cosmo could find what they needed, then Harley asked Sprocket to shine his light around the barrier.

"Barrier?" asked Cosmo.

"Grandpa Eden has a layer of plants to put the slugs off. He never harms creatures so tries to think of the best natural ways to deter them. He puts plants at the edges that the slugs don't like, so they turn around and go back outside instead of getting to the yummy stuff."

"That's so clever," said Cosmo, bending down to investigate. "Is this wormwood? And there are ferns … and spurge."

Harley shrugged. "I don't know the names,

but if we have a look at the edges, we should find a slug. Sprocket, shine your beams over here. Let's choose the largest one we can find."

They got down on their hands and knees and scoured the ground around the plants.

After a short while, Cosmo called out, "Here's one! I think it's heading for your grandpa's seedlings."

Harley hurried to see. She plucked it from a leaf. "Excellent. Here, open the bottle of super grow for me, please."

"Do you know what's in it?" asked Cosmo, doing as he was asked.

"Not exactly. It's a secret formula Grandpa Eden came up with to help him win the Forgetown summer fete best fruit and vegetable 'Super Strawberry' category. He's won it five years in a row now. But I do know it's all natural ingredients, so the slug should be perfectly safe." She carefully tipped a few drops on to the leaf, then put the slug on it. "We'll leave it overnight and come back in the morning. See you here at seven?"

Cosmo frowned, as though wrestling with his thoughts, then nodded.

The slug was already slowly chomping on the lettuce. They watched it for a moment, then Harley tipped several more drops on to the leaf. "There. Better safe than sorry; a fish told me that once."

"Harley! Are you in the greenhouse?" It was Grandpa Eden.

"Coming!"

She put the lettuce protector over the slug, grabbed a handful of strawberries from a nearby plant and pulled Cosmo outside.

"Ah, there you are! Cosmo's mum will be here in a moment. Have you been at the strawberries again?"

She popped one in her mouth and handed another to Cosmo. "It's not my fault if you grow such tasty things."

A loud rumble sounded along the lane and

the huge, shiny transport appeared, screeching to a halt outside Hitch House.

"Meet you here in the morning," Harley said, giving Cosmo a quick grin.

CHAPTER 10

SLUG

The next morning, after a restless night of tossing and turning, and thinking about her plan, Harley got dressed lightning quick and ate breakfast early. She hoped the slug had grown at least a bit. Perhaps it would only be twice as big, rather than three times.

She looked at the clock on Sprocket's side. Almost seven. Cosmo came running down the lane. She waved.

Just as Cosmo arrived, a huge crash sounded inside the greenhouse. They ran inside and stopped dead.

The slug was the size of a seal pup!

With a shiver of her shoulders, Harley said, "Yikes! I didn't think it'd get that big!" She picked up the rack of tools the slug had knocked over. After the initial shock of seeing it, she began to smile to herself. This was better than expected, wasn't it? It was a bit gross seeing a slug big enough to squash Sprocket, but then again, this slug would have no problem eating the fungus. She was going to save the Iron Forest! She might even become famous. She'd almost definitely win Pupil of the Term. "Best stay back a bit, Sprocket," she said.

Cosmo flapped his hands. "What are we going to do?" His voice wobbled.

"Don't panic, Cosmo. Let's think of it as an

unexpected advantage. This slug is going to demolish the fungus. But we need to get it to the forest, and fast."

"Harley, look at the size of that thing! I'm not touching it."

"It'll be fine." Well, she hoped it would. And in the meantime there was no way she was going to show the ever-worried Cosmo she was in any way fazed by it. "Fetch Grandpa Eden's wheelbarrow from over there. Angle it down and I'll roll it in."

"Is everything all right, Harley?" Grandpa Eden called from the kitchen window.

"Fine! I was just getting some strawberries for school and I knocked over a pot. Sorry!" She looked back to Cosmo. "We need to hurry, before he gets suspicious."

"Don't you think he might already think you're up to something?"

"Maybe, but that's not unusual, to be honest."

Cosmo tilted the barrow and Harley gave the gooey body of the slug a shove. It felt slimy and horrible as her hands squished into the flesh, but she pushed it out of her mind and thought about saving the Iron Forest, beating Fenelda and winning Pupil of the Term. After much shoving and grunting, the slug was in the barrow.

"To the Iron Forest!" declared Harley. She tried to pick up the handles of the barrow, but it was too heavy. "Cosmo, you hold one and I'll hold the other."

Cosmo grimaced, but he picked up the other side.

Then, panting and puffing, they made their way along the track as quickly as they could, stopping frequently to take breaks.

"I don't think there will be any officials

down here this early," said Harley hopefully. It would be hard to talk their way into the Iron Forest with a giant slug. They turned the corner and the forest came into view.

Sprocket stopped suddenly in front of them, his tail extending and pointing to the trees.

Harley's heart gave a leap. "Someone's down there. Look – coming out of the forest! Quick, get behind this bush."

They hurried and waited. The slug kept wriggling to escape, but Harley realized that if she stroked its back (which was totally disgusting), that seemed to calm it. She looked through the branches as footsteps approached.

It was Fenelda. She was carrying a jar with a sample of the fungus in it, which she stuffed into her bag as she turned the corner. *She must be planning on testing the fungus,*

Harley thought. Perhaps she already had a solution in mind. Harley's veins filled with fire at the thought of Fenelda's self-satisfied face if she was the one to save the day. Harley tightened her lips and imagined a swarm of ironsting wasps chasing after her enemy.

They waited a few more minutes to be sure Fenelda had gone before continuing on their way.

"Fenelda must be doing her own experiments on the fungus," said Harley. "Which is good, because it means she hasn't found an answer yet and we're a step ahead!"

After a jolty journey on the path down as gravity threatened to pull the barrow out of control, they reached the entrance to the Iron Forest. It was cordoned off with white-and-red tape and there were big signs that read

DO NOT ENTER.

They ducked beneath the tape, feeling a bit guilty, but determined, then pushed the barrow and slug to where they'd first seen the fungus. They stopped in amazement.

"Grandpa Elliot wasn't wrong! Look how many trees are covered now!" Harley's heart sank. It was like seeing a part of her home destroyed; all the happy picnics, expeditions to find parts for Sprocket, and trips with Grandpa Eden to find garden tools. She felt glad they were doing something to stop it. She couldn't stand by and do nothing.

They heaved the barrow towards one of the trees and carefully tilted it so the enormous slug rolled out. Harley and Cosmo watched with bated breath.

It didn't move.

"Come on, sluggy, breakfast time," Harley said optimistically, but as the seconds passed, her shoulders sagged. The slug didn't move. Had she got it wrong? Was the task just too big for two children to handle?

Cosmo looked at her. "What now?"

With a sudden ripple of its belly, the slug edged forward.

Harley's heart gave a little leap. "That's it, off you go!"

Slowly, the slug made its way towards the tree, paused, then began munching happily on the fungus.

"It's working, Cosmo!" She stared at the slug and a wave of relief and joy made her grin from ear to ear. "I can't believe it – I mean, I can, because we're, quite frankly, brilliant!"

"It really is working!" Cosmo smiled. He

pushed his hair from his face and tucked it behind his ears. His cheeks were flushed with triumph too. Or was it relief that Harley hadn't messed up? Whatever it was, it felt good to share this moment with him.

Cosmo looked at his watch. "We'd better get to school."

"Yes, come on, worrywart, let's get back. Sluggy has it all in hand now."

As they hurried up the steps at Cogworks, they bumped into Fenelda.

"What have you two been up to?"

"Nothing," said Harley, giving Cosmo a secret smile.

CHAPTER 11
THE MISHAP

Harley had tried to check the slug's progress after school the previous day and that morning, but found she couldn't get near the forest because of the officials hanging about at the entrance. She was planning to try again after school. She was desperate to see whether her plan had succeeded, though in the end it turned out she didn't need to visit the forest.

Harley was in a junk art lesson with

Professor Maple before lunch when something caught her attention outside: Professor Horatio was running up the path waving his hands.

"What in Forgetown has got into Professor Horatio?" asked Professor Maple, opening the window. "Is everything all right, Professor?"

He stopped and looked up. "Yes, Professor Maple, I do believe it is! I was just down in the Iron Forest, assisting the Horticultural Society in collecting yet more samples for tests in Inventia City, when I saw the most extraordinary thing!"

Harley's heart forced itself to the front of her chest. Could they have discovered the slug? She gave a quick glance in Cosmo's direction and stepped closer to Professor Maple.

"It's a miraculous occurrence!" Professor Horatio held his arms out as wide as they could reach. "What appears to be something I can only describe as a giant slug has been spotted! It's in the forest as we speak, eating its way through the fungus. It seems to be saving the forest!"

"Did you say giant slug?" asked Professor Fretshaw, who must have heard Professor Horatio and rushed from her office.

By now, the rest of the class was at the window, listening intently to the news. Even a few garden-bots who had been trimming the grass at the edge of the path had stopped work.

"The officials didn't notify us of any such plan? Where in all the furthest reaches of Inventia would they find a slug of that size?" asked Professor Fretshaw. Her face was scrunched up as though many questions were trying to escape.

Professor Horatio shrugged. "That's the strange thing. None of the officials know anything about it! But wherever it's come from, it seems to have stopped the fungus from spreading any further."

It was impossible for Harley to contain the enormous grin on her face. Her plan had worked! The Iron Forest was going to be all right. Should she reveal herself right now as the mastermind behind this?

Cosmo sidled up close and whispered, "You should probably go to Professor Spark at lunchtime and tell her."

Harley sighed. Yes, that was probably the sensible and mature thing, instead of running outside and blurting it out theatrically, which was what she wanted to do.

She turned to Cosmo and nodded. "You're

right. But you should take some credit too."
Then she noticed Fenelda staring at her, pinch-
faced, from behind him. Harley couldn't help
giving her a very small, smug grin.

After the Cogworks' clock chimed for lunch,
Harley and Cosmo hurried to Professor Spark's
classroom. She wasn't there.

"I wonder where she is," said Harley.

"Maybe she's gone to the Iron Forest to see
the slug for herself?" suggested Cosmo.

"Let's go and look for her," said Harley,
feeling like she was trying to contain a great
balloon of excitement that wanted to burst.

They didn't make it far. Professor Fretshaw
was in the entrance hall with Professor Spark,
who was holding a groaning ironhog.

Harley glanced at Cosmo.

"What happened?" asked Professor Fretshaw.

"I thought I'd take a look at what was going on in the Iron Forest and I found this poor fellow. It looks as though it's been attacked." She indicated the ironhog's side, where it had several large marks. "I thought at first it was another ironhog – although it's unlikely, as they are usually peaceful."

"A curious bite indeed," said Professor Fretshaw, examining it. "There are many small marks like rows upon rows of teeth, similar to..." She paused. "Professor Spark, are you suspecting what I am?"

Cosmo swiftly pulled Harley back into the corridor and said in an urgent whisper, "They're the marks of a slug!"

A huge wave of doom hit Harley. "But slugs

are harmless creatures!" she protested. Could it be that the slug had gone rogue? She didn't want to believe it was true. That would mean she was responsible.

Cosmo glared at her with eyes like transporter headlamps. "Maybe they're not so harmless when they are the size of a seal! What if the slug got bored of eating the fungus and started attacking other things? And think about it, Harley, it's been feeding on fungus for over a day now – it's probably even bigger. We have to own up to this."

It was as though all the sunshine had suddenly been replaced by a great thundercloud. "But it might not be, I mean, we can't be sure," she stuttered.

"Harley."

"Maybe the ironhog was close to the

fungus and the slug accidentally caught it. Why don't we go down and check first, just to be sure?" But in her head, the thundercloud was spreading, because if the slug really was running rampant and attacking other creatures it would be a disaster, and it would be all her fault. Guilt was an iron ball in her stomach.

Fenelda Spiggot walked around the corner. They froze.

"Oh, hello," she said breezily, flicking her hair as she continued past.

Harley pulled Cosmo along the corridor, then out of the back of the school. They hurried towards the Iron Forest.

"Won't we get in trouble for leaving the grounds without permission?" asked Cosmo.

"Grandpa Elliot once told me that the Iron Forest was historically part of the school grounds, so technically we're not breaking the rules."

He looked at her doubtfully but swept after her like flotsam carried on the tide. When they neared, they arced around to avoid the group of officials gathered on the path at the entrance to the forest, then sneaked under the cordon tape. When they reached the area of fungus, sure enough, the giant slug was nowhere to be seen and the fungus was spreading again in great swathes of multicoloured, rippling fluorescence.

"Maybe it's close by, let's look a bit further," said Harley. It soon became apparent that the forest, usually full of birdsong and the snuffle of ironhogs, was utterly silent, and there was still no sign of the giant slug.

"Oh dear, this isn't good." Harley shook her head. Something that she'd meant to help was now making things worse than ever.

"Harley, it's time to own up."

She looked at Cosmo. "But maybe we can find it? Perhaps just another day to look."

It was as though Cosmo was drawing up all his strength to say his next words. He took a long breath and put his hands on his hips. "I'm sorry, Harley, but if you're not going to tell Professor Spark, I will."

A sinking feeling tugged at her chest. What would this all mean for the forest? She was certainly saying goodbye to Pupil of the Term now. She frowned angrily. "Fine, I'll go and tell Professor Spark."

They hurried back to Cogworks and started up the corridor in the direction of Professor

Spark's office, but before they reached it, the clipped voice of Professor Fretshaw rang out across the school speaker. "Would Harley Hitch and Cosmo Willoughby report directly to my office. I repeat, Har-ley Hitch and Cos-mo Willoughby!"

CHAPTER 12
THE WEIGHT OF DISAPPOINTMENT

As Harley and Cosmo turned the corner, they saw Fenelda waiting outside Professor Fretshaw's office. Harley clenched her fists to stop herself from running over to give her a good shove. She must have overheard them on their way to the Iron Forest.

Fenelda put out her bottom lip in pretend sympathy. "Oh, did you come up with another failure of an idea, Harley? What a pity. It's a good job one of us has a brain.

My idea involves starving the fungus of oxygen by using a felt wrapping. Professor Fretshaw has said she's going to pass it on to the Horticultural Society. A much more sensible solution than thinking you could use a giant gastropod." She let out an annoying, high-pitched snigger.

Harley barged past Fenelda and knocked on Professor Fretshaw's door, then went inside with Cosmo. Professor Spark was waiting too.

After the professors had questioned Harley on what Fenelda had told them, and Harley admitted it was the truth, Professor Fretshaw revelled in telling her exactly how disappointed she was, while being entirely unsurprised.

"I wanted to have you expelled, but Professor Spark has convinced me to be more forgiving because of your so-called well-meaning intentions. You are to carry out a term's worth of litter clean-up duty with detention every day for two weeks. But if you so much as step out of line, you'll be expelled faster than a firework on Inventia Celebration Day. Do I make myself clear?"

Harley nodded. Cosmo received less punishment, just a week of detention and clean-up duty, as Harley insisted she was to blame, but Professor Fretshaw was clearly still very angry with both of them.

When they were dismissed, Professor Spark escorted them out of the office. "I applaud your keenness, I really do, but it was severely misguided. Harley, you should have come to me with your idea, and, Cosmo, I'm surprised at you; as a new pupil I would have thought you'd have been a little more –" she thought for a moment "– a little more cautious."

They both stared at the floor. Harley couldn't believe how it had all gone so wrong. She knew Grandpa Eden would be upset that her actions had caused harm to other creatures in the forest, and Grandpa Elliot would be cross that she'd lied to them. She'd let them down. She'd let the Iron Forest down. Things were worse than ever.

Professor Spark sighed. "Off you go to your lesson."

As they let the spiral stairs transport them up the tower, Harley turned to Cosmo. "Detention and picking up litter isn't so bad. It could've been worse, I suppose."

"Worse?" Cosmo said with a quiet fury that surprised her. "The whole school knows me as a troublemaker, and all I ever wanted was to keep my head down! I wish you'd never been late that first day, then we wouldn't have been forced together in the first place. I tried to warn you about your plan, but you wouldn't listen. I think it's best if we stay away from each other."

At the top of the stairs she watched him stomp ahead. She'd been trying to stay calm until now, but Cosmo's outburst made the feelings surge out. "Fine! I didn't need you as a friend anyway."

When Harley finished school, her grandpas were waiting for her at the gates. They'd received an urgent transmission from Professor Fretshaw, so Grandpa Elliot had left work early and Grandpa Eden had abandoned his greenhouse chores, and they'd come straight to the school for Professor Fretshaw to update them on the situation.

They hurried home in awkward silence,

then sat down in the living room.

"What were you thinking?" said Grandpa Elliot.

Grandpa Eden shook his head. "You should have asked my advice about your idea and the super grow!"

Usually Grandpa Eden could be relied on to be more forgiving. She didn't think she'd ever seen him so cross. How could she have messed it all up so badly?

"I'm sorry, I just wanted to… Never mind."

"And did you even consider what introducing a new predator might do to the ecosystem of the forest?" asked Grandpa Eden.

Looking at her boots, she shook her head.

Grandpa Eden sighed. "I believe Professor Fretshaw has given you a suitable punishment?"

She nodded and bit her lip, suddenly feeling

overwhelmed. "Can I go to my room now?"

"Yes, of course," said Grandpa Elliot.

The next day at school, Harley could feel the weight of everyone's stares. Cosmo refused to make eye contact with her and he had requested to move seats. Professor Spark had swapped him with Letti so that he was now beside Fenelda, who was taking every opportunity to tell him that she had told Professor Fretshaw it was entirely Harley's fault.

Harley didn't mind taking the blame – it had been her idea, after all – but she had thought that perhaps Cosmo wouldn't be so cross today, that they could at least still be friends. For some reason, not having Cosmo beside her made it all feel much bigger than any of her past mishaps.

Even worse, almost no one would speak to her. She heard whispered conversations that would stop when she was close, about how their family's jobs were at risk now that things in the Iron Forest were escalating, and that Harley had made it even more serious. But Harley couldn't help thinking that at least she'd tried. The Forgetown officials still hadn't found a way to stop the fungus.

During the lesson, Letti kept giving her sympathetic smiles and told her in a whisper that she'd heard Professor Horatio inform Professor Fretshaw that despite their best efforts, no one could catch the giant slug. "Apparently it's taken a liking to cogweed and fuse-ferns and there's hardly any left. And they can't find it because it's become expert at hiding."

Harley was feeling more alone than ever, and even Sprocket couldn't lift her mood. She went for a walk with him around Forgetown after school, but seeing Mr Bobbins hang his CLOSED UNTIL FURTHER NOTICE sign outside Cosmic Sewing and old Mrs Fig struggling to walk without her motor-driven skate frame made Harley so depressed that she decided she needed to talk to someone who was outside of everything. There was one place she knew she could rely on. She hadn't been there in ages.

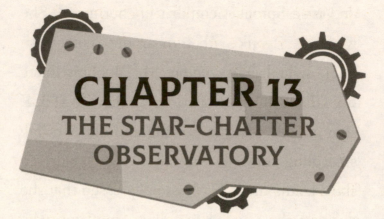

CHAPTER 13
THE STAR-CHATTER OBSERVATORY

The star-chatter observatory was on the opposite hill to Cogworks. It was a beautiful, glass-domed structure at the top of a tall tower. There was something about space and the stars that fascinated Harley. A sense of freedom and possibility, a place where there were so many questions yet you didn't feel that you had to come up with the answers.

Harley asked Grandpa Eden to drop her off. He gave her a hug before she went inside.

"I don't deserve that," she said.

He sighed. "We all make mistakes and learn from them. It's part of being human. Grandpa Elliot and I know you're sorry and that you had good intentions. But don't worry, someone will find a solution for the fungus. And the slug."

She gave a sad nod, then climbed the spiral steps with Sprocket.

Dr Orbit was at one of the telescopes dressed in a long leather coat and scarlet waistcoat. He looked over and smiled widely through his brown beard, which trailed like smoke to his waist. Harley was always impressed by how many tools he had attached to his belt: small spheres, an astronomical pocket watch, mini-telescopes and the like.

"Harley! Great to see you. You're right on time. Alpha Centauri has just thrown Pollux across the sky. Something about invading her space." He shook his head. "Honestly, leave them alone in daylight and they run riot. Can you have a look at the eastern skies while I take care of them? Ursa Major is being a total diva; I'm running out of patience, but she likes you."

Harley knew that Dr Orbit must know about her forest capers, but appreciated he was being just the same as usual. She sat in the seat of the large telescope pointing west. It felt nice to be somewhere she didn't have to face people judging her for what she'd done. She moved the telescope across the evening sky, becoming absorbed in the vastness and beauty, and allowing herself to forget about all the gloom that she'd been feeling. She tracked her coordinates carefully until she saw the flamboyant star dressed in an all-white ball gown, with lots of sparkle and feathers.

"Well, hello, dahr-ling! You're just in time to hear my rehearsal. Dr Orbit has no appreciation of the arts. But first, tell me, how are you? You look sad. Of course, we've been watching events unfold, but why don't you tell me about it yourself?"

Harley recounted everything that had happened. "It was awful, the worst day ever! How am I going to put this right?" She still couldn't believe that within the first week of a new term she'd managed to cause so much chaos. And that she'd managed to make a friend and lose one in the same time too. She felt another pang of sadness as she thought of Cosmo.

"You could try singing it out?" said Ursa Major brightly.

Harley wrinkled her nose.

"Come along. Take a breath, warm up with me, me meeee meeeee..." Ursa Major sighed. "Harley, your heart isn't in it today. It's like everything is out of sorts, and I don't mean just you. There are those strange lights in the Iron Forest, for a start, and that figure that keeps lurking around there."

"That would be Fenelda Spiggot," said Harley resentfully. "Always sneaking around where she's not wanted."

"Hm, maybe. But what would she be doing in the forest at night?"

Harley shrugged. "She followed us the day we first found the fungus. She's always snooping, looking for chances to get me into trouble or to make herself look good."

"Hold on, let me call Proxima Centauri; he saw it too. Oh, Proximaaaaa!" she sang out

across the night sky. A dazzling star in a blue
diamanté dress appeared.

"Ursa, how are you? Mwah, mwah. Oh,
hellooo, Harley."

"Hello, Proxima," Harley said sadly. It was
lovely to see the stars but she still couldn't
shake the cloud of gloom.

"My, my, you have quite lost your dazzle, haven't you?" he said.

Harley put her head in her hands. "Why did I ever think that a giant slug was a good idea?" She should have listened to Cosmo, done more research, but she'd been too distracted by her worry about the Iron Forest, wanting to fix things straight away. And, of course, wanting to win Pupil of the Term had been part of it too.

Ursa Major reached out her arms. "Harley, dahr-ling, if I could come and take it all away, I would. But I can't." She turned to Proxima. "Sweetie pops, you were with me when we saw the figure in the Iron Forest, weren't you?"

"Yes, we were rehearsing our duet for the upcoming Celestial Soirée, when something caught our eye. It was down by the strange, rippling lights."

"Maybe it was my giant slug?" Harley shrugged.

"No, it was definitely walking," said Proxima.

"Harley thinks it might be that Fenelda Spiggot," said Ursa.

Proxima shook his head. "Most definitely not. I distinctly remember being drawn by a rather loud argument she was having with her brother that same evening about who could have the tidy-bot to sort their room out first."

"That makes sense." Harley gave a laugh despite herself. "She's not the sort to tidy it herself!"

"No, and the figure in the forest had a brassy glint about it," said Ursa.

Harley lifted her shoulders back. Perhaps there was more to this; if it wasn't Fenelda, then who was it?

"We may not have the answers, but we can give you advice," said Proxima. He nodded at Ursa.

"Proxima is right. You know what they say, Harley."

"What who says?"

"All the great stars, of course!"

"What do they say?"

"The show must go on!"

"What do you mean?"

"Things have gone wrong. But it doesn't mean you can't keep going and fix it."

Sprocket licked Harley's arm.

"Harley, finding solutions is what you do best. We've never known you to give up."

She smiled; with their distance and observations, the stars made the truth seem clear somehow. She'd gone about it all wrong. Cosmo had tried to stop her, but she hadn't listened. She'd been determined to do it her way.

But the stars were right: even though she got things wrong sometimes, she always tried her best, and she wasn't going to stop now.

Harley looked at the two stars in all their sparkle and glamour gazing down at her. "Come on, Sprocket. It's time to find the solution."

CHAPTER 14
PLEASE AND THANK YOU

The following day was Saturday, so after an early breakfast, Harley left a note for the grandpas to say she was going to meet Letti, then hurried to the Iron Forest with Sprocket. She hated lying to them, but she had to try and right her mistake, even though she risked getting kicked out of school for good, if she got caught again. With a renewed sense of determination, she'd not gone to sleep until she had a plan; it was simple and involved a large rope and a bag full of strawberries.

Her heart sank as she reached the Iron Forest. It was a depressing sight. There were now many notices saying DANGEROUS and some more tape blocking the path, all put there by the Horticultural Society. She ducked beneath the tape.

"We'll draw the slug out, tie it to a tree, then send an anonymous message to the Horticultural Society to say it's been captured." She looked at Sprocket, who tilted his head. "It's the best idea I can think of."

Sprocket nodded.

But before she'd even started, she noticed a few trails of lettuces and various slug-tempting foods had already been left on the ground.

They looked as though they'd been there a while. With a sinking heart she realized that if it hadn't worked for the officials, it wouldn't be likely to work for her, tempting as Grandpa Eden's year-round strawberries were. She'd need to come up with a better plan.

She trudged a little further into the forest, thinking. As she walked, Harley noticed something shiny on the ground. "Be careful, Sprocket. There must be oil pods around." She paused; there was something different about this oil. She took a closer look. It wasn't as dark or gloopy as the oil from the pods. She moved to another patch. "Look, there's more over here … and here. There's a trail." It led away from the devastated patch of trees and deeper into the forest. "Come on, Sprocket." A glimmer caught her eye. "More fungus! And it looks new, because it's only a small patch at the moment, but there is a big patch of the oil here, and it's leading in the direction of the junkyard." Her heart thumped. She wondered if this had something to do with what the stars had seen: the mysterious figure in the forest.

When Harley and Sprocket reached the junkyard, the trail kept going. Sprocket gave a quiet bark. His tail pointed into the trees. Harley crept forward. She put her finger to her lips. There was talking beyond the patch of trees at the back of the junkyard. Harley could just make out some strange shapes and structures, and it sounded as though someone was giving a speech. She gestured to Sprocket to be quiet and edged forward on her hands and knees into the trees.

Many robots of various shapes and sizes gathered in a clearing beyond that was surrounded by tents. A robot with a square head and spiral springs for hair addressed the others. "The Iron Forest has been cordoned off, but the fungus still thrives. It is advancing strongly on its own, so we don't need to plant any more."

Harley couldn't believe what she was hearing: robots had been putting the fungus in the forest! She bit her lip, feeling confused.

"Too long have robots been taken for granted by Inventia."

The other robots nodded in agreement. Harley was sure she recognized a few: the every-help-bot that met Fenelda after school and a couple of the tidy-bots from Cogworks.

"I would enjoy a *please* once in a while," one called.

"I like cleaning, but a *thank you* every now and then would be nice!" said another.

Harley frowned; they had a good point. While she and her grandpas were always kind and grateful to robots, as were many people in Forgetown, she had witnessed lots of people who weren't. Like Professor Fretshaw and Fenelda – people who didn't treat robots with the same respect as fellow creatures. She patted Sprocket on the head. He was a companion, not a thing.

"We need fair treatment for robots!" called the robot with the spiral spring hair, who Harley realized must be their leader.

"Woof!" barked Sprocket, joining in.

Harley's heart leaped into her throat. "Sprocket! You weren't meant to reply! I mean, you're right, but you've kind of given us away."

Sprocket gave an apologetic whimper, but now all the robots were looking their way. Harley considered running, although she didn't fancy her chances against all these robots. She knew every-help-bots could travel speeds of up to twenty miles per hour. And, well ... she couldn't help feeling a little curious, so she stood still and allowed one of the larger heavy-duty lifting robots, with clamps for hands and rolling feet, to lead her from the trees into their clearing.

"Who are you, snooper?" said the robot with the spiral spring hair.

Harley took a breath and drew her shoulders back. "I'm Harley Hitch. But who are you? Why are you all hiding out behind the junkyard, and what have you been up to? I can see you're upset, but how is destroying our beautiful forest going to help anything? It'll only make people angry when they find out what you've done."

The robot observed her curiously and looked down at Sprocket, who was peering out from behind her leg. "Are you a friend to robots?"

Harley nodded. "Of course."

"And how do we know that?"

"Yes," called a robot from the crowd. "We

can't trust humans."

"She must prove it," said another.

"How can I prove it?" Harley said, frowning. She'd never had to prove her friendliness before. What a strange test! She shrugged. "Kindness is something you just … do."

The robot leaned closer to her. "Then just do some."

Harley looked to Sprocket, who tilted his head. She wondered what would happen if she couldn't convince them. There were an awful lot of them. How could she do kindness? Worry was like moths fluttering in her belly. She thought about Grandpa Eden and Elliot and the sorts of things they might do if she'd had a bad day.

"I could make you all a nice hot cocoa?" she tried.

Sprocket whimpered disappointedly.

"Oh! You don't drink, that was silly of me! I wasn't thinking." She looked about and saw a broom resting beside a pile of junk. She grabbed the handle. "Here, let me sweep up for you."

The broom rumbled and pulled away from her hands. "Hey, I was having a nice power nap!" Two mechanical eyes stared crossly at her from the brush.

"I'm so sorry, I didn't realize you were a robo-broom!" Harley said, her cheeks filling with embarrassed warmth. Why did she keep making silly mistakes when she was trying to do something nice? She'd never convince them she could be trusted at this rate, and she needed to if she was going to get them to work with her to find a solution and stop the destruction of the forest.

Sprocket let out a woofy snigger. A few robots joined in, then more, and soon they were all laughing, including Harley, who couldn't help feeling relieved.

"All right, young human," said the spiral-haired robot. "My name is Rebelina. I'm the leader of this camp. Take a seat."

A small robot nudged a crate towards her and Harley sat down.

Rebelina looked at her suspiciously. "How did you find us?"

"I followed a trail of oil. I thought it was from a pod plant, then I noticed it was lighter, more like the oil my Grandpa Elliot uses on Sprocket's joints." Harley noticed a trickle running down from Rebelina's knee.

"My foot got tangled in some cogweed yesterday and I fell," said Rebelina when she saw Harley looking. "We don't have the tools to repair it here."

"We have plenty of tools back home. We can help you."

Rebelina frowned, as though she wasn't used to being offered help. "Thank you."

Harley leaned in. She needed to ask more about what the robots had been doing, but she could see she had to tread carefully. "So … you're behind the fungus in the Iron Forest?"

Rebelina nodded.

"May I ask why?"

"We're fed up with being taken for granted by the people of Inventia City. Many of us are treated without respect, or a word of kindness. I've had enough of being asked to chop and prepare every meal for my human without ever receiving a thank you."

"That's awful!" Harley patted Sprocket's head. They had been together ever since she was a baby; he knew everything about her, had been there for her first steps, made her feel better when she felt alone or scared. And she knew that helped them be close friends.

"All we want is to be treated well and for a bit of thanks for the roles we play."

"Of course," said Harley, nodding in agreement. Though it still didn't seem right that the forest was suffering.

"We decided to make our voices known, so we left our positions and set up camp here."

"You definitely have a point. But I don't understand how planting fungus in the Iron Forest is going to help your cause. Surely you've seen the damage you're causing? The forest is dying!"

"The city relies on the Iron Forest to get new robot parts and the fungus is stopping that. When the city can't make any more robots, then they will realize how much they need us."

Harley thought for a moment. She could understand what the robots were trying to do, but as she'd learned from the slug incident, sometimes when you were angry or excited or worried, you didn't always make the best decisions. "Rebelina, you are right to be upset. But did you stop to think there might be a better way? The fungus is slipping out of control. If it kills off too much of the Iron Forest it might never grow back."

Rebelina let out a sad-sounding bleep. "It is a little more active than we thought it would be. We wanted to make a point, but we do not want the forest to die. I have been thinking we must own up to the problem."

A seed of a plan was fizzing inside Harley. She hadn't found a way to fix the giant slug and the fungus yet, but this was something she could help with. "I'm sure there's a better way to handle this, and I think we might be able to do it without everyone blaming you and the whole situation getting worse. Will you promise not to come forward for now?"

Rebelina nodded. "You have a better way?"

"Will you give me a couple of days? Promise you'll stay out of the forest for now?"

"I like you, Harley Hitch. You understand and are kind to your robot dog. All right. I will give you two days."

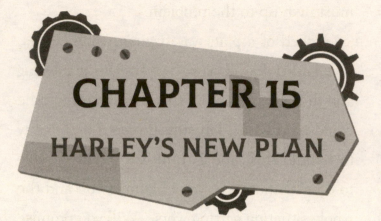

CHAPTER 15

HARLEY'S NEW PLAN

For a brief moment after leaving the robot camp, Harley thought about running to Cosmo's house on the way home ... before she remembered they weren't friends any more. She missed having someone to share secrets with.

It was lunchtime when she arrived home and her grandpas were setting the table. She took a long breath before entering the dining room, knowing they were going to be cross with her for going to the Iron Forest again. But she needed their help if she was going to get things right this time. Over lunch, she told them about Rebelina and the other robots.

"I want you to know that I'm trying to make up for everything."

Grandpa Elliot crossed his arms and frowned deeply. "Harley, you went to the Iron Forest again, after you'd been warned how dangerous it was?"

"I did, and I'm sorry, but I need to put things right. Haven't you always taught me to take responsibility for my actions? And this time will be different because I'm asking for your help."

Her grandpas exchanged glances.

"It's true," said Grandpa Elliot. "We've always told you not just to say sorry but to be sorry through what you do. OK, Harley, what are you suggesting?"

Harley thought for a moment. "It might be better if people don't know the robots are behind the fungus, in case it makes them angry. I think there's another way. It's down to us to make some noise; we need to tell everyone how the robots are feeling, and fight for their rights." She looked to Grandpa Elliot.

Grandpa Elliot had a twinkle in his eye as he looked at Harley. "I do believe I know what you are about to suggest."

"Do you?" said Grandpa Eden. "Because I haven't got a clue."

"Will you do it, Grandpa Elliot? Write Rebelina's story for the *Forgetown Daily*, about how they've had to run away because they are so unhappy. Once people know how sad they are, I'm sure people will sympathize. Maybe we could campaign for some sort of official act, so everybody has to treat the robots fairly."

Grandpa Elliot smiled. "Great idea, and I think we can go one better. My old university friend, Daphne Cringle, works for the *Inventia City Times*. She owes me a favour." He walked over and put a hand on Harley's shoulder. "I can't promise anything, but I will do my best."

Harley smiled, feeling hopeful for the first time in ages.

"In the meantime, I'll head over to the robot camp and see if there is anything they need. It can get cold and damp at night and it'll be playing havoc with their joints," said Grandpa Eden.

Harley nodded. "The leader, Rebelina, has an injury you could fix."

Grandpa Eden poured some tea, then raised his eyebrows at Grandpa Elliot. "And there's that other small matter you were going to talk to Harley about."

"What's that?" she asked.

"Ah, yes. The officials are getting closer to finding an antidote to the fungus. They are hopeful of testing it in a week or two. In the meantime, they have been using felt wrapped around the trees to try and suppress it."

Harley frowned. That had been Fenelda's idea. She was glad it was helping the forest, but the thought of being happy about an idea of Fenelda's was like being asked to bite into an onion. "And is it working?"

"A little, but it's taking time and it's not enough," said Grandpa Eden. "But what I wanted to talk to you about is the giant slug.

It's still on the rampage, and while it's keeping the fungus at bay in parts, it's causing more damage all the time … I'm afraid the officials have decided that the only way forward is to exterminate it. They are sending for specialists from Inventia City. They'll arrive on Tuesday morning."

Harley's chest squeezed tight. "They want to kill it?"

"I'm afraid so. They think it's the only way to stop it hurting the forest. It's destroying the ironhog and velocipede habitats, and it's munching its way through everything it can find."

"I went over there to catch it earlier, but I realized my idea wouldn't work … and then the robot trail distracted me."

"How were you going to catch it?" asked

Grandpa Elliot.

"A strawberry trail and some rope, but they'd already tried that and failed. I need to be more inventive."

"And I suspect the slug has grown too large to be contained by a rope. I think you'll need another way," said Grandpa Eden.

Cosmo flashed into Harley's thoughts. She'd been wrong not to listen to him. She'd felt angry and hurt that he hadn't wanted to be friends after everything, but she had to accept responsibility.

"What is it, Harley?" asked Grandpa Elliot.

"I was thinking of Cosmo. He's good at ideas too, but I didn't listen to him when I should have."

"It's important to admit when you're wrong," said Grandpa Elliot.

"I'm going to save the slug and the Iron Forest, and I'm going to apologize and make it up to Cosmo." Even if he didn't want to be friends, at least she'd have said sorry. "And when I think of an idea, I promise I'll run it past you both first."

With a smile, Grandpa Elliot passed Harley a chocolate chip bun. "You get thinking. In the meantime, I'll speak to Daphne Cringle and we'll see if we can help those robots."

CHAPTER 16
THE IMAGINARIUM

Despite spending the whole of Sunday trying to think of solutions, Harley had no idea how to go about catching an oversized slug. Grandpa Eden had been right: a rope on its own wasn't enough. She needed to think of something, but her mind felt like tangled wool.

At lunchtime on Monday, Harley hurried

to the Imaginarium, a large space in the upper dome of Cogworks where pupils could go to think, create and imagine outside of the classroom. Most pupils were still a little frosty with her, but Rufus had flashed her a sympathetic grin and Letti was being nice, so it wasn't all bad.

Fenelda was there, sewing large pieces of felt together with Cosmo. It made Harley's stomach do a little twist to see them together. It was a bit of a surprise, but then Fenelda had probably done it just to annoy her.

"Oh, hello, Harley," Fenelda said snidely. "We're helping with the Horticultural Society's effort to stop the fungus by wrapping the trees in felt. My parents are working with Cosmo's mum and they say the best way to get noticed for Pupil of the Term is to support the collective effort, rather than take heroics into your own hands."

Cosmo's shoulders tightened.

"What are you doing?" Fenelda asked Harley pointedly.

Harley picked up a box and placed it in the middle. "Sometimes you have to think outside of it."

"Outside of what?"

"The box."

"You're thinking outside of the box?"

Harley nodded. "You should try it sometime." She noticed the flash of a small grin on Cosmo's lips, which made her feel hopeful that maybe, in time, they could be friends again.

"You really are something else," said Fenelda, then glared at Cosmo, who looked back to his sewing.

Harley ignored Fenelda and sat down, cross-legged, trying her best to block out everything around her.

So, how to catch a slug… Fenelda gave a little cough. Harley wished she could stick Fenelda in a dark hole and forget about her. How was she supposed to concentrate when— Wait, slugs liked the dark and the damp… That was it! She needed to create the darkest, dampest place in the Iron Forest. A trap of some sort. She had no idea how. She could probably cobble something together, but she only had a day and if she got this wrong then the poor slug, which was in this situation through no fault of its own, would be exterminated.

Fenelda sniggered, breaking Harley's concentration again. But it didn't matter now.

Harley already knew what to do next, and it was thanks to seeing Cosmo. She needed to go to the library and research it properly. But before that, there was something else she had to do. Taking a deep breath, she walked over to stand in front of Fenelda and Cosmo.

"Cosmo, I'm sorry for not listening before, and for not being more careful. I understand if you don't want to be friends, but if you do, I'm going to the library later to work out how to make things right, and I would very much like the input of someone I trust."

Fenelda sneered the whole time Harley spoke, and Cosmo shuffled his feet awkwardly.

"But, also, I'll understand if you want to be friends with Fenelda instead. She's much less likely to get you into trouble."

Again no one replied.

"I'll see you around, I've got to go." Harley walked away holding her head high.

After school, Harley hurried to Forgetown Library.

"Hey, wait!"

She turned. Cosmo was running down the path after her.

He stopped alongside her. "Sorry about earlier. To be honest, Fenelda keeps grabbing me to help her and I'd really rather not. What are you going to the library for anyway?"

"I thought I'd finally listen to you and research my ideas. I really am sorry, Cosmo."

There was an awkward pause and Cosmo started fidgeting his feet. "So do you mind if I join you?"

Harley's grin spread like sunbeams in the forest. "Of course you can!"

Sprocket gave a happy bark.

They carried on walking together while Harley told him all about the robots and then the plan to exterminate the slug.

"I know just the book to help. After you told me about the natural barriers your grandpa Eden uses, I looked them up, you know, just for fun."

They found the book in the library and researched the most effective and humane traps for slugs.

"There's just one problem," said Cosmo. "These are traps for normal slugs."

Harley smiled. "We need to scale it up and I know just the place. Cosmo, it's time for you to meet Rebelina."

They hurried to the junkyard. "Rebelina, this is my friend Cosmo." Harley and Cosmo exchanged a look and grinned. Yes, *friends*. That's exactly what they were. It felt good having a friend at her side.

Harley explained what they and her grandpas were doing to help the robots and the situation with the giant slug. "We need a large metal shell and something that I can put a layer of water in."

"There is an old transport that will be perfect," said Rebelina. "I will gather the robots to take it down for you."

They took the transport shell to the Iron Forest, upturned it and closed all the doors and windows so the slug couldn't easily wander back out, filled the bottom with water and soil, then covered it with a layer of the dead branches and leaves so that it was dark inside.

"There. What giant slug could resist?" said Harley, tipping a large bucket of leafy vegetables and fruit, which Grandpa Eden had given her, into the corner.

CHAPTER 17
COSMO'S PLAN

It was a fitful night's sleep for Harley, worrying and hoping that the trap would work. She would feel dreadful if the slug was killed because of her. In the morning, she went down to the trap with Cosmo and her grandpas. Harley peered inside, and to her delight and amazement, the giant slug was sleeping in the corner.

"Excellent work, Harley," said Grandpa Eden. "I knew you could find a way to start putting things right."

They all stared at the slug. It glistened in the gloom and was plump as a giant's overstuffed pillow, certainly much wider than before, but perhaps not quite as long.

Slugs were not something Harley would usually pay much attention to, but she felt huge relief that they'd caught it and could save it.

"What now?" asked Cosmo.

Grandpa Eden looked at Harley. "How does it look compared to when you first fed it the super grow?"

"It's certainly fatter, but it's maybe a little smaller in length," Harley said.

"That's good. We'd expect it to be fatter with all the overindulging it's been doing, but if it's reduced in length there's a chance the super grow will wear off and the slug will return to its normal size over time. Until then, it will need to go on a careful diet, and you'll need to provide controlled conditions to ensure it doesn't inadvertently harm anything."

Harley's eyes widened. Was Grandpa Eden

suggesting what she thought he was suggesting? "You're not… You don't mean… I have to look after it, like a pet?"

Grandpa Elliot nodded. "Grandpa Eden and I stayed up late constructing an enclosure around the back of the house – just in case the trap worked."

"A pet slug?" Harley said again, strange visions erupting in her imagination as she thought about how she might take it for walks and play games with it like she did with Sprocket.

A small snigger escaped Cosmo's mouth. "I'm sorry, Harley. It's just the thought of a giant pet slug."

She let out a giggle too. "I'm never going to live this down at school!" But she was so relieved they'd managed to catch the slug that she felt like she could put up with anything.

She looked over at the creature, who was now awake. It sucked up a whole melon as easily as a grape. "Well, sluggy, it looks like you're stuck with me for a while."

"Come on," said Grandpa Eden, patting her on the shoulder. "Let's get it home."

Harley suddenly remembered the robots. "What about Rebelina and the robots?"

"The article will be out today in Inventia City, and the petition for a Robot Act has been launched," said Grandpa Elliot. "Their plea for politeness will be listened to, and hopefully become part of Inventia law. And no one need know about their connection to the fungus; they'll believe it was just a strange variant brought in on the wind."

"That's great," said Harley. "But we still

need to get rid of the fungus that's here. Do the officials have any solutions? Grandpa Eden, have you heard anything from your friends at the Horticultural Society?"

"It could take a while, I'm afraid. The officials in Inventia City are still testing their potion."

"But the fungus will have spread even more by the time it's ready!" said Harley, deflated. If something wasn't done sooner, what would happen to the forest?

"I've been working on something, actually," said Cosmo, taking a piece of paper from his pocket. "I've been doing some research of my own at the library, looking for a solution to the fungus, some sort of natural liquid to make it retreat. I think I've found it, I have all the ingredients listed and amounts, I just need some help getting hold of them and with the brewing."

Harley smiled. "I know just the person. You'll help, won't you, Grandpa Eden?"

"Of course. But really we should pass the formula on to the officials."

"Won't it just get delayed in their testing procedures?" said Harley.

"Most likely," agreed Grandpa Elliot, frowning.

They all thought for a moment.

"Did you say it was all natural ingredients?" asked Grandpa Eden.

"Yes, I'm very interested in organic solutions," said Cosmo.

"That's good. Perhaps if we made some quickly, we could simply test it out – just a little bit at a time, nothing too risky..."

"That's after we've taken your new pet home, and sent you two off to school," added Grandpa Elliot.

Harley cracked her knuckles and took the handles of the wheelbarrow. "Come along, sluggy."

After putting the slug safely into its enclosure back at Hitch House, Harley and Cosmo hurried to school, accompanied by Sprocket. They made it through the gates a little before nine o'clock.

"Just in time," said Primbot. "Please be aware that officials will be onsite today to close off access to the Iron Forest."

"Close off?" asked Harley. Her heart thumped.

"It will be officially closed at dusk after

they've caught and killed the slug. There will be great penalties for anyone going in after that."

Harley exchanged a worried glance with Cosmo. How would they be able to test the potion if the forest was closed? She bent down to Sprocket and whispered, "Hurry back to Grandpa Eden and tell him he has to get the potion finished by the end of the day. It's our only chance."

Sprocket barked and bounded back down the lane.

In their lesson, Professor Spark approached Harley and Cosmo. "What is it, you two? You've been looking out of the window all morning. Are you feeling sad for the forest?" she sighed. "I know I am. But I'm glad to see you're friends again."

To Harley, it felt right to tell Professor Spark

at this moment. She looked at Cosmo and knew he was thinking the same. They gave each other a nod, and proceeded to explain about the potion. The rest of the class fell quiet as they listened in.

When they'd finished, Professor Spark looked thoughtful. "I've known Eden for many years, and his skills at brewing garden remedies are second to none. If Cosmo has come up with a formula he thinks might work, then we should try it. The officials are tying themselves up in knots and it could be too late before they get it right."

"Exactly!" said Harley. "The forest could be destroyed by then."

"Let's hope he can get it made in time." She smiled at them both. "Right, everybody, back to work, please."

By the end of the day, word of the plan had got around the whole school. When the Cogworks clock chimed three, Harley and Cosmo rushed to the school gates, along with the rest of the pupils and all of the professors, in the hope that Grandpa Eden would be there.

But there was no sign of him. All Harley could hear was the swift pumping of her heart in her ribcage. She had her fingers crossed so tight she couldn't feel them. A few pupils began walking down the path to go home. Harley's shoulders slumped.

Professor Fretshaw said something quietly to Professor Spark.

Harley tried to ignore her, but then Fenelda pushed herself between Harley and Cosmo. "You just love the spotlight on you, don't you, Harley Hitch?"

Then a barking sound echoed up the lane –
it was Sprocket! He bounded around the bend,
followed by Grandpa Eden and Elliot pushing
a barrow with big buckets in it. Harley's heart
soared.

"You did it!" she cried, running towards
them.

"Steady on, Harley, we need to see if it
works," said Grandpa Eden.

The professors and a large group of
interested pupils gathered by the Iron Forest.
There was also a group of officials with chains
and fences, having been informed by the
grandpas that the giant slug had been caught.

"Hey, we're about to close the forest!" one of
them called.

"But it's not closed yet!" said Grandpa Eden.
He looked to Harley and Cosmo. "Quick, take

the potion and try it."

Everyone watched as Cosmo and Harley hurried into the forest with the wheelbarrow.

"Mind those oil pods," Harley said quickly.

They curved around them towards one of the nearest trees covered in fungus, then took out their brushes and began painting the formula over the patch. Everyone fell silent as they watched.

Harley held her breath and focused on the fungus. "Please work, please work," she muttered soundlessly.

A minute passed, maybe two. Then a small bit of the fungus suddenly stopped rippling with colour. Harley blinked to make sure she wasn't imagining it. The motionless area slowly spread until the whole zone they had been painted gradually began fading and retreating.

"It's working!" said Cosmo.

"If anyone could get it right, it's you," said Harley, nudging her friend. She couldn't believe they'd done it! She turned to the crowd of pupils and professors behind them. "I would like to let everyone know that this formula was all worked out by my friend Cosmo Willoughby."

Cosmo retreated behind his long curly fringe, but couldn't hide his wide smile.

Lettice Bigley began clapping, followed by Dolores Dredge. Professor Spark joined them, Professor Fretshaw gave a grudging smile, and pretty soon everyone was applauding.

Apart from Fenelda Spiggot, who stormed forward.

"Hold on! How do we know it wasn't Harley's grandpa who came up with the formula?" The clapping stopped as everyone looked at Fenelda. "Perhaps they stole it from—"

"Fenelda, stop," said Harley.

"I will not stop!" shouted Fenelda, marching onwards.

"Nel!" called Harley.

But it was too late. Fenelda had walked straight into a patch of oil pods. As she stepped on one it squirted all over her pristine uniform. She yelped, then as she tried to leap away, she

223

slipped and fell face first, setting off a chain reaction of oil splats.

Harley shrugged and swallowed her own laugh. "I did try to tell you to stop, Fenelda."

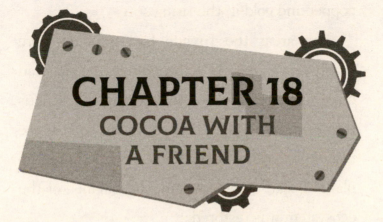

CHAPTER 18
COCOA WITH A FRIEND

The end of term was upon them. A layer of frost coated the distant rooftops of Forgetown and the great domed roof of Cogworks, and huge steel pipes chugged out soft puffs of steam. Harley made her way down the lane towards the Iron Forest for an early morning walk with Sprocket. The air was fresh and sweet with seasonal chill, and the treetops glistened with ice-dusted leaves. Cogweed and nail pines glinted silver, copper and gold in the rising sun.

The areas the fungus had infected were slowly recovering. As it turned out, the slug had done a pretty good job of keeping the fungus from doing too much damage, and as soon as the natural creatures of the forest returned and the plants began growing again, the balance of the ecosystem was restored.

For the robots, the newspaper articles had brought about an important shift in the way people viewed them, and the Robot Act had been put in place to make sure robots were well treated. Rebelina and her friends were free to return to Inventia City, although some, including Rebelina, decided to stay in Forgetown. Rebelina had told Harley that she felt bad about taking such extreme action with the fungus and wanted to quietly go about making amends. She was helping repair all the postal pigeons and regularly heading down to the forest with Daisy the mechani-weather-bot to check on the recovery of the plants and trees, and to give them an extra sunshine boost along with some of Grandpa Eden's wonder fertilizer. Others had taken positions such as helping at Kitchen Imagine, where they were launching their new mechanical spaghetti spinners, or at the One-Hop Transport Shop fixing the variety of transports that were now able to be mended as supplies were returning.

After her walk, Harley arrived home to grab her school bag. She was just heading back downstairs when there was a knock on the front door.

"It's for you," called Grandpa Elliot.

Harley rushed down to see Cosmo standing

there. His uniform looked less neat these days, as he had added some new pockets and tool chains.

"You made it through your first term, then." Harley smiled.

He nudged her. "Just!"

They walked to school with Sprocket, who left them at the gate. Inside, the pupils gathered in the main hall. The professors stood at the front, and Professor Fretshaw held a cushion bearing the gleaming light bulb badge.

Once everything had settled down after the Iron Forest Mishap, as it had become known, Harley had performed well at her various Cogworks assignments, but Fenelda had too. After a few other small troubles this term, including accidentally gluing her sleeve to the table in junk art, and an explosive incident with a pumpkin in Professor Horatio's lesson, which absolutely weren't her fault, Harley was pretty sure she wouldn't get Pupil of the Term. But she found that she didn't mind. Having Cosmo as a proper friend and being in Professor Spark's class meant she'd had her happiest start to a year so far at Cogworks.

"Without further ado, it's the moment we have been waiting for," said Professor Fretshaw. "I am pleased to announce..."

Harley saw Fenelda twitch, ready to rise.

"...the Cogworks Pupil of the Term is someone who has fitted in extremely well to life at Cogworks, showing themselves to be hard-working, committed to doing the right thing, always thoughtful and diligent in their approach, and they played a big part in resolving the Iron Forest Mishap too. It is, of course ... Cosmo Willoughby!"

There was a thunder of applause and cheering. Harley had expected to feel a bit disappointed at losing out, but all she felt was bursting pride for her friend. He deserved Pupil of the Term more than anyone she knew. She nudged him and he looked back at her, mouth wide open in shock.

She smiled. "Get out from behind that fringe and go and collect your badge!"

His face lit up with a huge grin and he

made his way to the stage. Letti gave him a double thumbs up and Rufus patted him on the back as he passed. Fenelda joined in with the clapping, although Harley noticed it was stiff and her lips remained tight. Once onstage, Professor Spark beamed at Cosmo while Professor Fretshaw presented him with his certificate and pinned the gleaming light bulb badge on his waistcoat lapel.

With a small nod to herself, Harley knew it was where it was meant to be.

After school, Harley, Sprocket and Cosmo sat in their winter coats on the bridge across Rusty River. Small patches of ice floated along, but Harley was still hopeful they'd catch something.

A new flap opened in Sprocket's side and a tap appeared.

"What's that?" asked Cosmo.

"A modification Grandpa Elliot and I have been working on." Harley took two collapsible cups from her pocket and popped them open. She placed one under the tap and steaming hot cocoa poured out. "Thank you, Sprocket," she said, passing it to Cosmo.

"Wow, that's brilliant. Sprocket, you are the best robot pet ever!"

Sprocket's eyes flashed with hearts.

"I've not seen that before either!"

"It's a way for Sprocket to let me know if he's happy," said Harley, patting him on the nose. "After talking to Rebelina and the other robots, we decided to install something so Sprocket can tell us if he's cross or annoyed too. Show him, Sprocket!" His eyes flashed with lightning symbols.

Cosmo flinched, then he and Harley laughed as Sprocket swiftly changed it back to hearts.

Harley poured her own cocoa and the two friends sat sipping their drinks, their fishing lines dangling in the slow-moving water.

"Harley, what are we fishing for?" asked Cosmo.

Harley shrugged. "Let's just do it for fun today."

After a minute, her line pulled, and she

reeled in a flat fish. It stared at her, then opened its mouth and said, "Fall into the pit and gain your wit."

She frowned. "What could that mean?"

"I guess it means that if you get things wrong, it's all part of learning and knowing better next time," said Cosmo.

Harley shrugged. She couldn't argue with that.

"That works for me too. I've learned that sometimes a little risk is needed," said Cosmo. "If I hadn't taken a chance with my potion, the Iron Forest might have been damaged beyond repair."

Suddenly, Cosmo's line tugged. "Hey! I got one. I actually caught my first fish!"

"Excellent. Reel it in!" said Harley.

It was a small minnow. It cleared its throat,

then said in a very large voice,

"Strangers are just friends waiting to happen."

Harley smiled and looked at Cosmo. "They really are." His golden light bulb badge gleamed in the sunlight.

Sprocket barked in agreement, opened a flap in his back and popped up a large chocolate muffin to share.

Harley smiled. The school year so far had been nothing like she'd hoped, but it had been so much better in unexpected ways. And as for Pupil of the Term?

There was always next time.

ACKNOWLEDGEMENTS

I'm forever grateful to so many who continue to support my stories and imagination. Thank you to my second-to-none agent, Kate Shaw, and the wonder team at Scholastic UK: Lauren; Harriet; Bec; Pete; the sales, marketing and foreign rights teams; and editor Linas Alsenas for championing this idea and for always being my very best partner in stories. Hugest thanks to my editor for the project, Jenny Glencross, whose astute eye helped me bring details alive and get inside Harley's wonderful mind – you were such a joy to work with, and I'm so proud of our Harley! A big hooray to George Ermos for bringing my imaginings to the page with his wonderful illustrations (and for beautifying my map sketch!) – it's wonderful to have our names together on the cover. I also owe a huge debt to Scholastic designer Jamie Gregory for his (always) phenomenal vision and design work.

Thank you to the Bounce team, the booksellers, bloggers, librarians, educators, fellow authors and general book lovers who continue to support my stories and bring them into young hands. You are enormously appreciated.

Lastly, to the young readers, I wish you a warm welcome to the world of Inventia. With her inquisitive mind, determination and flair, Harley is a character who brings a big grin to my face while I'm writing. I hope she does for you too.

If you're ever in doubt, I recommend that you look to the stars or head to the Rusty River (but it's probably best not to go the pet slug route…).

Vashti Hardy is the author of *Brightstorm* and *Wildspark*. *Brightstorm* has been translated into several languages, was selected for Independent Booksellers Book of the Season and Primary School Book Club Reads, won the West Sussex Children's Story Book Award and was shortlisted for the Waterstones Children's Book Prize, Books are My Bag Awards and Leeds Book Award. *Wildspark* was the winner of the Blue Peter Book Awards Best Story 2020.

vashtihardy.com
Twitter @vashti_hardy
Instagram vashtihardyauthor

George is an illustrator, maker, and avid reader from England. He works digitally and loves illustrating all things curious and mysterious. He is always trying to incorporate new artiness from the various world cultures he reads about and explores.

Twitter @georgermos